FIGHTING RAMROD

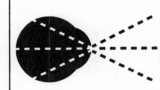 **This Large Print Book carries the Seal of Approval of N.A.V.H.**

FIGHTING RAMROD

Lee Floren

Thorndike Press • Thorndike, Maine

Library of Congress Cataloging in Publication Data:

Floren, Lee.
  Fighting ramrod.
    p.   cm.
  ISBN 1-56054-639-5 (alk. paper : lg. print)
  1. Large type books. I. Title.
  [PS3511.L697F5   1993]   92-43520
  813'.52—dc20   CIP

Thorndike Large Print® Popular Series edition published in 1993 by arrangement with Dorchester Publishing Co., Inc., New York City.

Cover design by Studio 3.

The tree indicium is a trademark of Thorndike Press.

This book is printed on acid-free, high opacity paper. ∞

FIGHTING RAMROD

ONE

Before the Corporation had bought the Bar T, the ranch had been run in a somewhat leisurely but competent manner. Wagons had lumbered out on roundup in the spring and fall and, when the spring roundup wagon had worked a certain area of the immense ranch, all the calves in that section had been branded before the wagon had moved on — regardless of how many days it had taken to run the wild calves out of the brakes and the high buckbrush.

But the Corporation was a group of wealthy Eastern men who knew nothing about operating a cow-outfit, but who had definite ideas on how the ranch should be run — most of these ideas being impractical and worthless. Matthew Kalin, millionaire head of the Corporation, said a ranch was only a business, nothing more — it *had* to be run efficiently because it *had* to show a profit.

Blustering and domineering, Matthew Kalin knew not a thing about running a roundup wagon, nor did he know the type of range over which the Corporation's newly-bought herds grazed — the ranch, to him, was just an area of soil shown on the map in his office, there at the home ranch. Spring roundup had to move along and move fast — it took money to run a roundup, and the sooner it was over the sooner some of the hands could be laid off. Therefore he had allotted three days to working the Wishing Hills section. The wagon worked the range in three days — but the circle riders had not run in all the calves. And, when the wagon had moved on, a number of "slicks" were still in the rough brakes.

Now Carl Hudson — range-boss for the big outfit — was running a cow out of the brush and silently cursing the Corporation for not giving his men more time to work this area. Had this time been allotted he and his partner, Shorty Madlin, would not now be running down these wild calves and branding them.

The cow had twin calves. The roundup crew had missed her and her two new offspring, and now it was up to Carl and Shorty to rope the calves, tie them down, build a branding fire, and put the Bar T iron on them.

They had jumped the cow back in the deep buckbrush around a spring. Her calves had been bedded down in the tall grass and she had been grazing on the greenery around the edges of the waterhole. The cow snorted and wheeled on seeing the two Bar T riders come into the small clearing. She started out on the

8

dead run, tail up and horns laid back, and then she remembered her maternal obligations — for she was leaving her calves behind. So, she wheeled again, head down, and tried to hook Carl's horse, but his horse, being an old well-broken cow-horse, leapt to one side, making her horn miss his forepart.

"We got to get them down on the level, Shorty," Carl Hudson hollered. "Not even room enough to wind up a catchrope here in this brush."

By this time the cow and her two calves were pounding through the high brush, heading for the flat area into which the coulee ran — about a half mile away, Carl figured. And behind her and her calves thundered Carl Hudson and Shorty Madlin, ropes in hand, loops built and ready to make their casts — when they reached the area that had no brush.

Carl Hudson rode high on his stirrups. He wore leather shotgun chaps that hugged his legs like steel casings, their tough bullhide turning the brush and its thorns. His horse packed a leather breast-shield fastened to the martingale and this piece of thick leather kept thorns from tearing the horse's breast. Carl Hudson was twenty-six and he was tall and bony. For five years now he had been range-boss for the Bar T. Hudson knew cattle and he knew how to handle men. He joked and laughed and rawhided with his crew, but when the chips were down he could become tough. He never asked a man of his to do something he himself would not do. He could fight with his fists and fight with his short-gun and his rifle — but he disliked fighting and he hoped he would never have to kill a man. He was a hard-working man and he wanted to hold onto his job, and he liked the respect and wages he got for being the tough range-boss of a hard bunch of cowhands. But he wished now that the Corporation had given him about a week longer to run out the Spring roundup wagon.

Two days for the Myers River country and three days in big Jonathan Basin — one day for Willow Creek, three days for the Wishing Hills. And so it had gone — a brutal thing, drawn up by a man who had known nothing of the terrain, the brush, the rough Wyoming weather, the rain, or the tough slants and the badlands.

Matthew Kalin had made it a point to be at the Bar T during the roundup, which had just been finished two days ago. Not *finished*, in the literal sense of the word, though; rather, the wagon had pulled into the big ranch on time, and, according to Kalin, that was all that counted. He had not known about the many calves the circle riders had missed in their haste to obey the schedule.

"Good work, Carl," Matthew Kalin had said when, at dusk, the roundup crew trekked into the home ranch. Riders were dusty, unshaven and saddle-tired. The canvas tops of the wagons were gray with ugly dust. Riders sported beards and were hollow-eyed and most of them swore that never again — as long as the Corporation owned the Bar T — would they ride for that outfit. But Matthew Kalin had not been dust-coated. He wore a loose blue suit that did much to hide his big belly and his face was plump and clean-shaven, the whisker-roots blue against the baby pinkness. He had rubbed his fat hands together and his narrow, thick-lidded eyes had held the speculative squint that a gopher has when he rears his head out of his hole and looks at a new garden. "You see by now, I am sure, that a ranch is like any other business. Has to be run efficiently and speedily to insure a profit for its owner or owners."

Carl had almost made an angry reply. But he caught himself in time — he needed his job.

Fact had been that he had not been paying much attention to the Eastern money-bags. For Matthew Kalin's daughter, Birdie, had stood behind her fat father. And Birdie had winked at Carl.

11

That wink had been deliberate and slow, and it was tantalizing. It seemed to say, "Tell him to go to hell, Carl," and, for another moment, Carl almost fell to the lure, again catching himself in time. So he did not tell Matthew Kalin to go to hell, and Birdie had frowned and pouted — she had frowned very prettily and her pout was also very lovely.

Birdie was blonde, and she was just twenty, and rumor claimed her father had almost bodily toted her out of New York City to keep her out of trouble. Birdie was an inch over five feet and she had her curves in the right spots. Her eyes were blue, but Carl Hudson had noticed one thing about those eyes. They were very hard to read. They were very, very changeable. One time, those sky-blue eyes might be dreamy, a lazy sleepiness in their depths; the next moment, they could be serious, and this dreaminess would then be gone. Lately, though, Carl had noticed, so he thought, another thing about those lovely eyes — they could be scheming, also.

He had never made a move toward Birdie or given her anything but a joking word. At the present time, women had no place in his plans; in fact, one of them might break his plans to smithereens. Also, Birdie was not for him or a man of his class — she was the only child of a millionaire, and she moved in circles totally alien to those of a range-boss, circles that would remain forever alien. Therefore he had stayed shy of Birdie.

So had most of his crew. They were drifters, men of the saddle, and their women were not millionaires' daughters — their women stuck around saloons and in the red-light districts. A few had played up to her and had got exactly nowhere, and some kidded Carl about her slyly, for she seemed to seek out his company, and she winked and joked with him — just as she had winked at him now, merriment on her lips and in her eyes.

Birdie had wanted to see a roundup in operation. Therefore, against Carl's wishes, she had started out with the crew. The first day out she had ridden circle with Shorty Madlin. Shorty had sported a smile as long as wagon's end-gate and had ridden out with a reckless Sioux warwhoop on his lips. But the next day she had ridden circle with tall Mike Hendricks, who then had the smile but neglected to give with the warwhoop.

And little Shorty Madlin, who now was whooping at the cow with the two calves, had worn a long face — a face so long he could walk on his chin.

On the third day Birdie had said, "Now I ride circle with you, Carl."

The cow darted to the right, the calves following her, and Carl's horse swung out, heading her and pointing her down the slope again toward the flat where they would rope the calves and brand them. His mind went back to the scene with Birdie Kalin and he grinned even now at her anger.

"You won't ride with me, Miss Birdie."

"Why not?" She was suddenly icy. She was hard and stiff and her blue eyes were slate gray now.

"You're just not going to ride any more on this roundup, that's why."

"And for what reason, range-boss?"

Carl had grinned, not liking one iota the task ahead of him. "Well, if you gotta know the truth, guess I might tell it to you, at that."

"Tell me."

Carl had kept on smiling, but the smile had not been genuine. "You raise hell with my crew. You ride with this man — and he's all smiles — and the rest are like a bunch of whipped puppies — they moan and sulk. A woman has no place on a roundup. When a man wants to swear, he has to look around to see if you are in earshot; these men should joke and make horseplay — but they don't, because they just watch you."

"Oh, so that is what is bothering you!"

"Yes," Carl had said, "that is it."

Her chin had gone up. She spoke in short

words. "You can go to hell, mister. My father owns over fifty percent of the stock in the Bar T. I can stay with this roundup as long as I want . . . Hey, take your hands off me, you big human ape!"

"So I'm a monkey now, huh?"

Carl had bodily lifted her into her saddle. She had kicked and squirmed and had tried to hit him but he got her between horn and cantle and got the reins in her fist. She had felt nice and soft, despite her anger and her harsh words. She had glared down at him. Then she had looked at the crew that stood and watched with deadpan faces and in silence. She evidently realized then she was making an ungraceful spectacle of herself.

"I'll be glad to go, Mr. Sour Mug," she had said. "I thank you very much for your hospitality and I am sorry I called you an ape. I should not have insulted the ape family. Instead, I should have called you a jackass."

"Thank you, young lady."

Then she had hissed like a big cat. She spat at him and missed him only because he jumped hurriedly to one side. Anger then flooded him but she was gone — her horse ran as fast as he could run, and she was laughing back at him. And then the crew had laughed, and that did make Carl Hudson see red.

"Man, she was mad clear through — what

will ol' Kalin say when she reports this to him?"

Carl was afraid of that angle, too, but it did not show in his voice or actions now. Maybe he had overstepped his authority. He had laid his hands on the big majordomo's only child.

But evidently Birdie had not told her arrogant, heavy-set father about the incident for Carl heard not a word of it from Matthew Kalin. But after that he kept shy of Birdie as much as possible. The second day after the roundup wagon had lumbered into the home-ranch he had been in the blacksmith shop fitting shoes on his horse, Gray Blanket. She had come in while he had been pounding a shoe into shape on the horn of the anvil and the first thing he knew her sweet voice had purred, "Well, lover boy himself, huh?"

He had turned, looking at her. She wore a print housedress that clung to her ample figure and she looked smaller than ever, even though she wore shoes with rather high heels.

"Now look," he had pointed out carefully, "I don't want no trouble, Miss Kalin."

"Birdie is the name, remember?"

"No matter what your name is, I just don't want no trouble."

"Oh Carl, how awful." She frowned prettily. "Am I really — trouble?"

Carl was having a bad time of it; he was

aware he was damp under his hat's sweatband and he knew the weather had not suddenly got any hotter. He heard boots coming and he was very glad when Shorty Madlin walked into the shop and said, "Howdy young lady."

Birdie had visibly scowled as she said, "Hello, Tall Man. You shoeing a horse, too?"

Shorty struck up a conversation with her but Carl noticed she entered the banter reluctantly. Another thought came to the long-geared range-boss — Shorty always wanted to be close to Birdie. Mike Hendricks also had contracted the disease.

Carl figured she was just a city flirt who liked to make men mad over her. Not that he did not like to be flirted with — he was a mere male with a male's deep vanity. But he did not like to be made a fool.

So, to save himself trouble, to keep Shorty on the straight and narrow, he had put a pack-saddle on a mule, filled the pack-bags with grub and supplies, and he and Shorty had headed into the Wishing Hills country to run out calves missed in the "scheduled" roundup.

Shorty had almost bawled. "You'd best git some other cowpoke to go with you, Carl."

"What's wrong with you?"

"My liver — she's ailin' up on me, Carl. Does me bad to set a saddle. Jars my innards and my liver hollers. Pains me, too. Better

17

get Mike Hendricks to go with you — he's a whole man."

Carl had grinned impishly. "This news won't break your heart, Shorty. But I'm sending Mike Hendricks and Smitty out to work out calves we missed, too."

Shorty had watched him carefully. "You are, huh? Where you sendin' them two hellions, Carl?"

"Bog Springs. Be over there a week, at the least. Your liver is all right. Last night you sat up most of the night in that poker game."

"Won twenty-three bucks, too."

Shorty Madlin had grinned. Carl could read his thoughts. Mike Hendricks was his closest competitor — outside of Carl — for Birdie's gay smile and attention. Now Mike was going to be stationed at Bog Springs and the Springs were at least fifty miles away. He and Carl were going to work the Wishing Hills area. The Wishing Hills were a mere twenty or so miles away and they would be camping there for about only four days, but Mike Hendricks wouldn't be back to the home ranch for at least a week. That meant that when he and Carl finished their job in the Wishing Hills he would have at least three days with Birdie without Mike Hendricks hanging around.

So they had left the camp with the pack-mule trailing behind, hating to move any faster than a slow walk. They had made camp in the boulders around Washout Springs the first night and because of the high sandstone rocks the wind could not hit them. They picketed-out their saddlehorses and the mule, and Shorty cooked supper over the open fire. After they had finished their chuck Carl leaned back against a boulder.

Shorty scoured the frying pan with sand. "That Birdie is some heifer, Carl."

"Quite a lot of female," Carl said.

Shorty regarded the pan, eyes down. "She ain't for me or Mike Hendricks, though, she ain't, Carl."

Carl had looked at the runty cowpoke who still seemed interested in the bottom of the clean frying pan.

"Why do you say that, long one?"

Shorty had grinned, then. "She's not for me or Mike, 'cause she's got eyes for only one galoot, and his name is Carl Hudson."

Carl had said, "You're joking, Shorty. She's worth over a million bucks. She has a college education — or part of one, I guess. I went to the fourth grade. You run around like a man who is addled, pard."

"You're addled; I'm not."

Carl had said nothing more. He had leaned back and sucked his pipe. Birdie Kalin had money — far too, too much money. She was

19

an only child. Her mother, he had heard, was a semi-invalid, going in and out of expensive hospitals. When and if *Mister* Matthew Kalin died — and he had to die someday; even millionaires don't live forever — Birdie would be a very rich woman. And a domineering woman, too, he figured.

Hell, she wasn't falling for a two-bit cowpoke. Get those thoughts out of your stupid head, Carl Hudson! She can have her pick of New York money-men. This is a passing fancy with her, nothing more. She was the type who carried on a constant flirtation, he reasoned, and she had headed out for him because he had acted hard to get — then, once she had him on the hook, she'd wiggle the line hard and get rid of him, her conquest complete.

"Your liver," said Carl, "really and honestly must be bad, Shorty, to have such crazy thoughts."

"It ain't loco though," Shorty stubbornly maintained.

TWO

Carl had been thinking of everything and everybody but the two calves and Shorty had done most of the work hazing them and their angry mother out of the brush. Now the calves left the buckbrush and thundered into the clearing. Carl hollered, "I'll take the bull calf, Shorty."

"I'll lay my twine on the heifer," Shorty yelped, rope cutting sharp swift circles over his wide old Stetson hat.

Carl's gray leaped under the spurs, closing in on the running calf. His loop made five turns — sharp and hard — and then the lasso went out. For a moment, the loop was perpendicular, suspended in front of the lunging calf, who was trying to kick himself in the ears with his hind hoofs.

Into the loop went the white head.

Carl Hudson was not a dally man — he tied his twine hard and fast to the saddlehorn, running the rope under the fork to give his horse lower leverage on the manila rope. Gray Blanket, seeing the noose settle closed back of the calf's ears, stopped in his tracks, legs stiff. He stopped so fast he might just as well have

21

crashed into a stone fence. Even before the horse had skidded to a halt, Carl was on the ground, boot heels digging soil as he hit the sod on the run, pigging string in his teeth.

The calf thundered into the end of the rope. He tried to bawl and then the noose cut off his wind. From then on, he had a rough time.

The calf switched ends right now, hind legs straight up in the air. Then his head and his hind quarters swapped places and he landed on his back in a wind-jarring jolt that made him bawl again in pain. The fall drove the wind out of him with savage suddenness. Despite that he tried to get up, but Carl Hudson, by now, had run down the taut rope and was on the calf.

Gray Blanket inched back, keeping the rope tight. Gray Blanket was an old hand at this game. So was his master. Carl's hoggin'-string — a length of thin buckskin whang leather — made fast and circular motions. Within seconds, the calf lay there, three legs tied securely.

Carl straightened. He tugged sharply on the lasso and this was Gray Blanket's signal to move ahead and allow slack to enter the rope. Carl glanced at Shorty, who had roped the heifer with his first cast, and was now tying her legs, his back to Carl.

Shorty's back was also towards the mother cow.

By now, the mama cow had back some wind, and she was fighting mad. And it was Carl's roaring shout that warned the short cowpuncher.

"Look out, Shorty!"

Shorty had just finished his tie. He jumped to his feet and turned just in time to see the mad cow bearing down on him in her wild charge. But Shorty did not run — he was an old hand with mad mama cows. There was only one thing he could do, and this was to lie down and hug the good face of old Mother Earth, just like he would love to hug one curvaceous Birdie Kalin.

By lying flat on the soil, the cow could not hook him with her horns, for she could not bend her head low enough to get her horns in a hooking position.

Her nose hit him, then she kicked futilely at him as he lay on the ground. She jumped over him and her calf and then, thoroughly angry, she pivoted like an ungainly fat dancer and started for the short cowpuncher again.

But, by this time, Carl Hudson was again in his saddle. Using his spurs, he drove Gray Blanket in hard, the horse's left shoulder hitting the cow behind her shoulder, sending her skidding and bawling in surprise and pain.

The horse followed in, using his weight, and again he knocked the cow down. Carl had doubled the free end of his lasso and this beat on the cow's bony ribs like a Sioux Indian beating on his tom-tom. The cow had had enough — if not too much. She scrambled to her feet and broke for the brush, leaping wide-legged and bellowing.

Carl pulled in Gray Blanket, grinning widely. He rode back to where Shorty was rubbing the fine dust from his face and smiling. The cow turned, looked at them from the brush, but did not charge again.

Shorty brushed his shirt. It hadn't been washed for two weeks. "She got slobber all over my clean shirt," he moaned.

"You haven't had that shirt on more than two weeks, either." Carl Hudson spoke with dryness. "Before Birdie came to the Bar T it seems you used to change shirts about once a month, if my memory serves me rightly."

"It don't serve you rightly. Before she came I changed every month and one-half. Now I'm a clean young man — every two weeks, a new shirt."

"The power of love," Carl said. "You'll be washing your socks next."

"A cruel, cruel remark," Shorty said sadly, wagging his head. "Well, yonder is your bull calf; here is my heifer calf. Both of them tied up an' ready for the blisterin' end of a brandin' iron which is strapped to your saddle. Yonder is the mammy cow — humble and contented. Who builds the fire — me or you?"

"You do, of course."

"I built the last one back yonder when we branded them three heifers, remember?"

"Remember yourself, fellow — you build the fire. I'm the boss, remember?"

Shorty shook his head slowly. "Wish they would of made me foreman instead of you, Hudson, and I'd have guv you a rough time. All right, get down the brandin' iron, and I'll pick up some brush."

Shorty walked to the edge of the clearing and found some old twigs from the cottonwood trees and started to break them. Carl untied the stamp-iron from his saddle and he was starting to go across the clearing to where Shorty was building the fire when he heard a strange voice behind him say, "Cow thieves, huh?"

Carl Hudson stopped in his tracks.

Fear did not stop him; surprise put the brakes on. The voice plainly belonged to a woman. Had Birdie ridden out from the Bar T to see them?

He glanced at Shorty.

Shorty was gawking at the woman who stood behind him.

"What the . . . ?" Shorty's voice was a dismal croak.

"Cattle thieves, huh?"

The girl was small, about five feet, if that tall, and she had dark brown hair, and her hat was on her back, held there by the throat strap. Her face was tiny and dark complexioned and her lips were slightly open, showing white teeth. She wore a housedress that clung to her figure, accentuating the right curves. But it wasn't the housedress — or even the young strange woman — that interested Carl Hudson so much.

It was the two things he saw in her arms that provoked his interest. One of these things was a baby. He was a chubby, curly-headed boy of about eight months. The baby was under her right arm, hanging there and apparently enjoying this whole episode, grinning happily.

Under the other arm was a rifle.

Carl knew more about rifles than he did babies, and he was sure this was a Winchester lever-action .30-30 rifle. He stared and then he realized his curiosity had run away with him, and he closed his mouth. But here they were — he and Shorty — miles from civilization, and out of the brush walks a young woman — dark and small and lovely — carrying a baby and a rifle.

Carl finally had his tongue. "Who are you, Ma'am?" he asked. His voice sounded like it belonged to somebody else.

She did not answer that question. Instead she asked, "Are you two men stealing these calves?"

"What do you mean — are we stealin' these calves?" Carl spoke in a rough voice. "Cattle rustlin' is a serious charge, Ma'am — they've hung men around here for stealin' cattle, and we don't aim to get hung — just yet."

The baby boy, hanging over a capable sun-tanned forearm, looked from Shorty to Carl, and his chubby face seemed suddenly solemn and judicial. Carl noticed something else. The woman had the hammer of the rifle eared back. She had it under her forearm, too, and it pointed in his direction, and her forefinger was crooked in the trigger. Carl started to sweat.

"That rifle must weigh heavy on your little arm," the Bar T range-boss said. "Especially when you got your other arm weighted down with that heavy little son of yours, missus."

"He is not my son. He is my nephew. And I am not a missus, thank you. I am Miss Janet O'Reilly, sir."

For some reason, Carl was glad to hear that the baby was not her son, and he was also glad to hear she was unmarried.

Shorty had finally found his tongue. "Miss Janet O'Reilly, huh? Sure a purty name. But heck, you can't be Irish. Most Irish women have black hair or red hair, an' your hair is a purty brown color."

Janet O'Reilly gave him a look dripping scorn but Shorty Madlin just kept on grinning like a school kid who had just won a spelling-bee. She swung her gaze back to Carl Hudson, who was watching that finger around that trigger and who was not smiling. Then she looked at their two saddled horses.

"That gray horse wears a CH brand. That bay horse had the Circle Seven iron on his right hip. Those two calves belong to that Bar T cow back in the brush. If that isn't rustling calves, then I'd like to know what it is."

Carl said, "That gray horse is named Gray Blanket. He is my private horse so I branded him with my initials: C H. I'm the Bar T range-boss, Carl Hudson by name. That bay horse yonder is ridden by this good-looking gentleman, whose name is Shorty Madlin. The Bar T bought him about a month ago from some horse dealers that travelled through with a herd and we haven't had time to rebrand him with the Bar T. That should settle your doubts, Miss Janet?"

He saw the girl's shiny upper teeth chew hesitantly on a full bottom lip. She moved the baby's weight a little and the rifle swayed some and Carl again felt fear touch him. But with this fear was the original thought that had hit him when he had first seen her behind him. What was a young unmarried woman doing out here in the brushy wilderness with a rifle in her hand and a baby over her arm? Nobody lived here in the godforsaken silence of the Wishing Hills. Where had they come from and what were they doing here?

"My partner has a stamp iron on his saddle," Shorty said. "Go to it and you'll see it is a Bar T stamp iron. Against the law to tote a runnin' iron in the Territory. Rustlers has runnin' irons — with them they can make any brand — but a man can only make one brand with a stamp-iron. Ma'am, if you'll pardon my sayin' it, you sure are dumb when it comes to brands."

At this moment the baby boy had stood enough, evidently, for he opened his mouth until it was big and wide and he bawled almost as loud as had the little Hereford calf when Carl had thrown him.

Because of the baby, Janet momentarily forgot her rifle — she couldn't handle both the rifle and the child. As a result, the Winchester left her grip suddenly, for Carl had moved in and grabbed the .30-30. The hammer fell but the bullet ripped harmlessly into the sod.

The girl said, "You no-good rustler."

Carl tossed the Winchester to Shorty who caught it and kicked the cartridges out of it, the lever rising and falling. When the gun had been emptied the short cow-puncher tossed the rifle to the ground and then dug out his dirty bandanna to mop his forehead. The baby bawled like he was getting branded and Janet had her hands full with him, a sort of motherly care on her pretty face.

Shorty looked at his boss "A pretty woman and a ugly gun," he hollered. "Me, I don't cotton to that combination."

"Me, neither," Carl hollered back.

"That kid sure can yowl," Shorty hollered, louder than he had to be heard above the baby's crying.

Carl fell for the cue. He roared out loudly, "Almost as bad as a baby bull, he is — a bull gettin' dehorned."

"Now you can see what life with Janet will be like," Shorty bellowed back.

"Not for me," Carl hollered.

Janet set the baby on the ground. He started to crawl towards one of the calves. Carl grabbed him and headed him off, turning him toward his aunt. The baby sat down. He had on rompers and was barefooted. He stopped crying and looked at Carl for sometime. Carl looked back at him. Carl felt sort of good, the way a man feels when he sees a baby. Shorty moved over and squatted beside the little boy. The boy smiled and tried to rub Shorty's whiskers.

"Sure a nice little boy," Shorty said, smiling up at Janet. "You still look kinda mad, sister."

Carl said, "Keep on being mad. Maybe someday you'll think twice before coming up behind two cowpunchers and calling their hands. Someday a man will not know a woman is behind him and he'll turn with his gun out, Miss Janet."

The baby wanted the rifle. Carl moved in and took the rifle away from him. "That rifle is not for you, little man. That rifle is for big ladies like Auntie. Auntie has been readin' them Buffalo Bill Stories and every man to Auntie is a cow thief."

"Rub it in," Janet said savagely. "Make fun of me."

"You look even purtier when you are real mad," Shorty said.

Carl smiled. "Go fly off the handle, sister. Women do that most of the time anyhow, or so it seems to me."

Her anger left. Carl got the impression she got angry fast, then cooled off just as fast — and then forgot, not holding a grudge. Which, he reasoned, was a good trait in a woman, a man, or even a horse or dog.

"Now, Miss O'Reilly, can my partner and me go about our chores without you interruptin' us?"

"I was wrong — I guess."

Carl spoke to Shorty. "Give her back her rifle. I don't think she could hit the inside of a barn shootin' out with it. Give her back her baby, too. We got brandin' to do. We're cow thieves, remember?"

"Oh, sure, rustlers."

"You two go to hell," Janet O'Reilly said.

"Such terrible language," Carl scolded. "You'll learn that innercent little baby how to cuss."

They got the fire going and got the branding iron in it, entirely oblivious of the woman and child, watching the iron slowly heat.

Shorty whispered, "Wonder who she is, Carl? I know her name is Janet O'Reilly. But where did she come from? Women don't wander around this wilderness and them that do — and none don't — don't tote babies an' pack Winchester rifles!"

Carl shrugged. "You got me stumped," he had to admit.

"Ain't you — curious?"

Carl lied glibly. "Not a bit. But it sure seems to have you settin' on pins and needles, Shorty."

Shorty glanced at Janet, who was squatted

beside the baby. "The trouble with you, Carl, is this."

"What?"

"You're savin' money so bad and workin' so hard to start a cow outfit of your own, you ain't got time to look at some of the neat and nicer things in life."

"Like who or what — for instance?"

"You take Birdie now . . ."

Carl stood up, grinning. "You take her, Shorty. I got enough trouble in my life without listenin' to her tongue ramble on and on night and day." He turned around and looked at Janet and essayed surprise, acting as though he figured she had gone. "You're still here, eh?"

"Oh, you shut your mouth."

The baby sat and watched in silence, eyes wide. To the baby the world was new and big and full of odd things.

Carl asked, "You're from the East, huh?"

"What makes you think that?"

"Oh, just a thought."

"I'm from Illinois."

"Nice state," Carl said. "I was born in Ohio."

"Oh."

"Where is your saddlehorse?" Carl asked.

"I walked over here."

"Walked?"

"Baby and I were out looking for a choke-cherry clump with a lot of chokecherries. The chokecherries will be ripe in a month or so, I guess."

"About a month. Service berries will be ripe in a few days."

"When the cherries get ripe we're going to pick a lot of them and make jelly and preserves and maybe some syrup."

"Do you live around here — close like, Miss Janet?"

"Yes, about a half mile. Just around the toe of the hill there, to the west."

"Never knew a soul lived around here," Carl said. "We worked this country on calf roundup a week or so back but never got into this section, I guess. You ain't livin' alone, are you?"

"No, I'm not. I said this was my nephew. His father is my brother, John O'Reilly, and then there is his wife — and I. We're home-steading in this area. We only came here a week ago," the girl said.

Carl nodded. Maybe that accounted for their settlement not being sighted by a Bar T rider. They had not been in this area when the Bar T wagon had zipped through. This was getting more complicated each moment. Carl built a mental map in his mind. The town to Sulphur Springs was about fifteen miles to the north.

About that, as the crow flies across country. He had heard that a railroad — the Grand Western — had recently laid rails into Sulphur Springs. He did not know — he had not seen the rails — he had just heard this from a drifting cowpoke. His outfit did not trade at Sulphur Springs. Their trading post was to the south in Willow Bend. Willow Bend was about eight miles from the home ranch. Since the Corporation had acquired the Bar T goods were sometimes bought in wagon lots wholesale in St. Louis or Chicago, shipped to a railhead, then freighted by bull team into Willow Bend. Sulphur Springs was too far away from the home ranch.

Carl Hudson had heard something else, too. He had heard rumors that farmers would follow the rails west. Already some farmers, so he had heard, had settled around Sulphur Springs town.

They had come in on the Grand Western. They had shipped in from back East and from the midwest states. They had ridden in on boxcars with their wives and children and relatives and with their household effects and their farming equipment and their stock — their horses and cattle and goats and chickens and dogs and cats. But this had not, so far, been of any concern to the Bar T outfit. Bar T range ran no further north than the northern edge of the Wishing Hills. There it bordered the range of another big spread. This was the Circle R outfit. Farmers — nesters, the cowmen called them — had settled on the Circle R range, so Carl had heard. Now the news — that a nester family had moved in on Bar T range — was somewhat of a shock to the range-boss. This seemed to be a nice little dark-haired girl. She had a pretty baby of a nephew. Undoubtedly her brother and her sister-in-law were nice people, too — Carl Hudson's type of people — hard workers, asking only a chance to work for what they wanted. But still, they had located on Bar T grass.

Carl Hudson knew a little bit about the law. The Bar T did not have deeds to the thousands of acres over which it ran its cattle and horses. The original owner of the ranch held his land by the theory of "squatter's rights." This meant that the first to come was the first to be served. He had been the first to "squat" on his sections of land. He had turned back the Cheyenne Indians, had helped kill off the "humpbacks" — the buffalo — and had turned cattle loose on these thousands of acres. Thus he had sold to the Bar T what right he had acquired through "squatter's rights." Congress had years before passed the Homestead Act. Under its provisions a man or woman could file on a homestead of one-hundred and sixty acres, or one-fourth of a section of land. The homesteader could also file for other "claims" — a hill claim, grazing claim, etc. All in all, he could hold a square mile of land, which was six hundred and forty acres, or a section.

After three years, he got final papers — he had to make some improvements, of course, before getting his deed from Uncle Sam. He had to build a house, break so much land to the plow and crops, and live on the land for a certain length of time. Then he got a patent, or a deed, to his land.

One farmer had fought a big southern cow outfit and had the fight taken into the territorial court where it was held that "squatter's rights" were not legal, and, to the amazement of the big cattle-kings, the cow business had taken a big stomach-hitting blow.

Some cowmen, those who read the handwriting on the wall, saw the end of free government range, and, accordingly, they settled cowpunchers on homesteads — filing on choice pieces of land around springs and waterholes and where there was grass to be cut for winter hay. These cowpunchers drew pay from their home ranch, did the work of cowboys, and lived on their homesteads to fulfill legal requirements, even to walking behind a plow. Then, when they received their patents from Uncle Sam, they signed these over to the cowman who, all the time, had paid their wages. In this way the big cowmen controlled choice areas and these areas, because of their strategic values, in turn gave them indirect control over fast-grazing sections of land.

Carl had heard that the Circle R was fighting the farmers and having a rough time. His mind went back to a conversation a few weeks ago with Matthew Kalin, right after the millionaire had come in from New York to "run" the round-up. Mr. Matthew Kalin had summoned Carl to his office, something the old boss had never done, or never would have done — he would have gone to the corral and talked with Carl. But Matthew Kalin looked upon all hirelings as mere hirelings, nothing more — and Carl had darned near not gone to the office.

Matthew Kalin had converted the living room into his office. He had been pacing the flagstone-covered floor — a short and heavy-thighed man with a cigar — when Carl had entered. Carl had not knocked. Matthew Kalin had looked up with a scowl. Carl thought the man might jump him about entering without first knocking, and Carl was just angry enough to wish that the man had.

"Carl, the Circle R, north of here, seems

to be having some trouble. These damned no-good farmers are moving in on their graze and running out their fences, building their houses, and taking up homesteads."

Carl nodded, saying nothing, knowing what would be next. And his summation proved to be correct.

"Are any of these nesters coming in on Bar T range, Carl?"

"Not that I know of."

"That you know of!" The cigar made impatient gestures, held by fat and pudgy fingers. "Look, man, you're hired to know about anything that happens on this ranch, on this range."

Carl had held his temper. He needed his job and he needed that twenty bucks extra each month he drew as foreman, for he had his plans. Carefully he had explained that this Bar T range was an immense piece of land, about sixty miles east and west, and about twenty or so north and south. That made about twelve hundred square miles of grass to patrol and account for.

"Well, do you know of any coming in on our grass?"

"I don't, Kalin."

Carl had deliberately not used the word *Mister*. He had wanted to get the old man's goat, and he remembered how the cigar had come up to be jammed between fat lips, but Matthew Kalin had said nothing. He had rubbed his smooth fat hands together, the sound oily and slick, and his flat lids had moved upwards, giving his pale eyes a hard and predatory look.

"When and if a farmer locates on our ranges report the event to me immediately, Carl. It's your job to keep them off the Bar T."

Carl had spoken slowly and clearly. "Bar T range is quite a distance from the railroad. They have to have rails close to ship out their products — their wheat and corn and oats and the likes. I doubt if any of them will move in on Bar T range. It would be a long way to haul crops into Sulphur Springs."

"We'll tolerate no nesters on the Bar T, Carl. The stockholders have much money invested in this ranch. We have to make it pay a good rate of interest. We can't do this if farmers occupy our grass." The fat hands had made a curt movement. "We have to have a good rate of interest on our investments."

Carl had left the company of the great Mr. Kalin without another word. Sometimes it didn't seem worth his while — even with the twenty bucks each month as a bonus. Now nesters had indeed moved in. And this one was right pretty, too — maybe even prettier than Birdie Kalin, Carl thought almost dismally. Now, as he branded the heifer calf, he had a deep scowl across his forehead.

The iron was very hot. It cut through the hair, leaving the stench curling upward, and it hit the hide. The heifer bawled in pain. The mother cow watched but did not charge. Carefully Carl burned the brand to his satisfaction, not too deep but just right. He had branded so many calves in his twenty-six years he was impervious to their pain. He handed the cooling iron to Shorty with, "Heat it up again and we'll make that other a Bar T critter."

Shorty restored the branding-iron to the fire.

Carl said, "Let it heat up a mite, son." He looked at his partner. "Well, it finally happened, eh?"

"Reckon so, and I don't like it one bit."

Janet was all ears. "What has finally happened?"

Carl decided to speak bluntly. There was no use in beating around the bush.

"Farmers has moved in on Bar T range. And our orders are to — well, all nesters . . ." He halted suddenly, becoming silent.

"What is a nester?" Janet asked.

She was dumb, Carl Hudson told himself again. No, not dumb — she just hadn't been in this area long enough to know all the vernacular.

"A nester, Miss Janet, is a farmer. Cowboys call them nesters because they build nests — they settle down, plow the land, make barbwire fences that cut range animals, and they raise crops — if it rains, if there are no cutworms, if the hail doesn't come, and if the grasshoppers don't beat their binders to the wheat. In other words, you and your family are nesters."

Carl saw color surge in and give her face a sharp prettiness. Her words, too, were sharp.

"You don't have to draw me a picture, Mr. Hudson. I know now what you mean. Well, let me tell you a thing or two, will you?"

"Shoot."

"We are here as legal residents, citizens of the United States. My brother had filing papers on his quarter of a section and my sister has also taken up a homestead next to his. And in a few days I'll be twenty-one and I'll file on a homestead, too, just as any citizen has the right."

Carl looked at Shorty. Shorty had a long and mournful face. Carl said, "The iron should be hot enough now, Shorty."

"Too bad," Shorty said, and he wasn't referring to the calf about to be branded, either.

He got the iron and branded the other calf. Then he untied the calves and they ran, tails up to their mother, who took them and wheeled with them, running out of sight in the brush.

"A couple of low-down sneaking cow-thieves," said Shorty sadly. "That is all we are, Ramrod Hudson."

"Low down and dirty," Carl mourned.

"But I read about people stealing calves — and I thought — and I — well, I read about it, in the weekly newspaper."

Carl asked, "Do you believe all you read, Miss Janet?"

"Are you trying to scold me, you long drink of water?"

"Water," Carl Hudson murmured. "Cold water, clear water, good water. I sure could stand a drink of water right now. Which reminds me that your farm must be right where thet good spring is, ain't it?"

"We filed on the land around the spring."

Shorty said dolefully, "I sure could stand a good long stiff drink." And he added, grinning, "Of water, of course."

Janet fell for their ruse. "Come along and drink the spring dry," she said. "And I'll introduce you to my family. Come, baby."

Carl had gained his point. He had wanted to look over the O'Reilly clan and see just what was what, and what kind of people they were. He had a feeling of despondency. When Matthew Kalin heard about these farmers

43

landing on the Bar T grass . . . and sooner or later word would get to the millionaire . . . well, there would be a fight, if the farmers persisted on remaining here in the Wishing Hills district. Carl did not look forward to fighting poor people. He hated to see open range go, but he figured it had had its day — all things had to go someday, and open range would disappear as people migrated west, which they were doing.

And Janet sure seemed like a nice girl. She made a nice picture carrying her little nephew, the lad braced against her hip. Carl and Shorty led their horses. The pack-mule was back in the camp in the rocks, about five miles away. They talked, the girl apologized, and the baby got heavier every step. Shorty noticed this and winced, wondering how a baby would look in his arms. He did not want to hold the baby. Carl wondered how a man held a baby, too. He wished the baby would grow lighter, not heavier.

Finally Janet said, "I have to stop. This kid is as heavy as a boulder. He'll grow up to be a bullheaded Irishman."

Carl said, "I'll take him, if you show me how to tote the little rascal." He hoped his smile was not too wooden.

"You don't know how to carry a baby?"

"I ain't never been married," Carl said

quickly. "And I've never been around where I could practice on a kid, either. He sure is a heavy bugger."

The baby liked Carl. Carl liked the baby. They got along right fine. In a short while he got over his embarrassment. He looked at Janet and smiled and said, "You know, I believe I'd make a good dad."

Janet didn't like the look in his eyes. She blushed and said, "Maybe so, fellow."

Shorty only grunted.

THREE

Things sure can happen fast sometimes, Carl Hudson told Carl Hudson. Here he was, walking into a nester's farm, a cowpuncher on foot, holding a pretty baby, a pretty girl walking beside him. A quick glance told him the O'Reillys had done a lot of work on their land since taking up their homesteads. They had a cabin up, made of cottonwood logs from along the edges of the hills. John O'Reilly was chinking up the spaces between the logs with a mixture of cement and mud and water. His wife, Patsy, was mixing the mortar with a shovel in a wooden box. The pair saw them coming and turned and stared. Carl noticed that a rifle was leaning against the raw logs in the new building.

Janet introduced them. "These two men work for the Bar T, folks." She told about her meeting with Carl and Shorty.

They shook hands. Patsy was a dark-haired, rawboned young woman, quick of manner and with flashing dark eyes. Plainly she would posess a tough temper and she was made of whalebone and would work until she dropped, Carl saw at a glance. He then turned his at-

46

tention to Janet's brother.

Carl handed the baby to the mother and shook hands with John O'Reilly. Janet's brother was a heavy-set man of around thirty, Carl figured. Patsy had acknowledged the introductions with a short nod that was not too cordial.

Shorty Madlin shook hands, too, and looked around. "You folks sure have done a lot of work to be here just a few days," he acknowledged.

"Got lots more to do," the farmer said slowly. He was feeling them out. They worked for his enemy. He was suspicious of them. "I got a barn to build and finish. But, got all summer to do that . . . won't need it until fall. More important I get our living quarters up and finished."

Shorty nodded respectfully.

"I'm ploughing about a hundred acres this summer, if I can get to it," the farmer said. "Going to let it lay idle and plant it to wheat early next spring. Season is too far gone now to do any planting, 'cept for maybe a little garden truck around the spring, where there is plenty of water."

Both of the cowpunchers agreed with this logic. They squatted, backs against the house, and let the shade feel good. Janet went to the spring and brought back a bucket of cold water

47

and the dipper went the rounds. Suddenly John O'Reilly leaped to his feet.

"Here we drink water, and I got some cold beer in the spring. Brewed it myself, and it's wild, but still tastes good. Janet, bring us some bottles, huh, sister?"

"Who was your slave last year?"

"You were, remember?"

Shorty Madlin's tongue came out and wet cracked lips in evil anticipation. Carl said, "Thanks a lot, mister," and wondered what the beer would taste like.

While Janet was gone, an aura of suspense and suspicion held the little group, the baby occasionally breaking it with his gurgles. But the beer turned out to be right good. They squatted and drank and sparred with words. Sooner or later, the main point would bob up its ugly head, but Carl was in no hurry — he wanted to see up this man and his outfit. They looked all right to him, but they would not look all right to Mister Matthew Kalin and the stockholders he represented. So he let John O'Reilly, in his due time and course, take up the matter that bothered them all, and this farmer did, in a short while.

"I've heard the Bar T is run by a bunch of bankers back East," the farmer said.

Carl nodded.

"I done heard that the big dome that owns

most of the stock was out to the ranch from New York?"

"He's out here," Carl admitted. "All two hundred and fifty pounds of lard is out here."

John O'Reilly had his beer sitting in the dust. He traced a ring around the base with his forefinger. Janet and Patsy, both holding beer bottles, sat on a box and watched and listened and were silent. The baby sat in the dirt and played. Finally he found a six-penny nail and he tried to put it in his mouth. His mother grabbed his hand and pried the nail loose but said nothing. Carl fingered his cool beer bottle and silently cursed his job.

For some reason the simplicity of this family scene touched him. This man had a good wife and a pretty sister and a nice little baby — he had something to work for and fight for. He matched himself against John O'Reilly. He was, of course, a few years younger — darned few, though. He had a few hundred bucks saved in the bank. He had a saddle, three head of private horses, horses he owned, and he had some old duds. Nothing more. He finally decided, out of this flash of thinking, that a man who lived alone was not much good, either to himself or to his neighbors. *An old bachelor,* he told himself, *is a sort of pathetic sight, and I'm becoming just that.* He had five more years to work — he had made this plan

49

— and then he would quit with a stake enough to buy some cattle of his own and go into ranching in a small sort of a way, but still independent of Matthew Kalin and his like, and his own boss.

He had thought over this homestead angle, mentioning his ideas to none of his cowpunchers — for they would laugh at him and think he was loco. But a man could get a nice hunk of land free and develop it. Get a homestead like the one these people had — land with water on it — and run cattle back in the brakes that would never be homesteaded because they were too rough for the plow. His thoughts were broken by the farmer's next question.

"How does them millionaires what own the Bar T look upon us homesteaders? By that I mean this: some big cow outfits is fighting us farmers. And I understand I'm settled on the north rim of land the Bar T claims but ain't got no deeds on. Federal land agent in Sulphur City warned me, but I wanted this spring — and besides, I'm here legally."

There the question was — it had finally been uttered — and it lay between them, awaiting an answer.

Carl slowly put his bottle down and glanced at Shorty Madlin. Shorty had a face as long as that of a hammerhead horse but his eyes were on his bottle.

Carl knew, without looking, that the two women were watching him, awaiting an answer. This was the tough part of this job: fighting two women. Fighting a man in this predicament was tough enough, but scrapping with two women — both pretty — and one unmarried — this would be hard to do.

But they expected an answer.

Carl glanced toward Janet, who met his eyes with a solemn face. She was lovely and she was worried. Carl saw that Janet's hands had calluses. Her fingernails were clean, but they had been worn down, evidently from working with the mortar used in the chinking.

But why did he notice such things?

"I can give you the answer only as Kalin gave it to me, O'Reilly," he said slowly.

"And how was that, Hudson?"

Carl said, "I hate to say this. You folks seem like nice people. But Kalin gave us cowhands strict orders to run off every farmer what dares to set a foot on Bar T range."

Well, there it was. Spoken out between them — ugly and mean. The Bar T legally owned not a foot of the land it claimed. But the Bar T had money and hands to back up their threats — and if worse came to worse, the Bar T would hire guns, law or no law.

John O'Reilly asked slowly, "Is that

an order, Ramrod?"

Carl got to his feet. "That's the way Kalin put it to me. I'm his range-boss. I only work for the Bar T. I don't lay down the policy. The stockholders do that and I have to carry out their orders — or bunch my job." He looked at Janet. "I'm sure sorry it turned out this way, Miss Janet."

John O'Reilly began, "I . . ." He never got to finish his sentence, whatever it had been. For Janet was on her feet. Her eyes were angry and they burned on Carl Hudson.

"You — you're cheap."

"In what way, girl?"

"You work for a big corporation that has no soul. You know, deep inside of you, that that order is wrong, terribly wrong. You know that! But still, you're so cheap you'll carry out that awful order, just to hold your job. Well, what if we won't move, Mr. Cowman?"

Carl did not feel too good. "That will be up to Kalin to decide what to do," he told the stony-eyed girl.

She opened her mouth and said, "You big cheap . . ." and then she snapped shut her mouth. "There is no use wasting good words on the likes of you." Her teeth came down again, white against her red bottom lip, and she looked at Shorty, who did not meet her gaze, and then she looked at Carl, who also looked away.

Then, skirts rustling, she turned without another word and, her nephew on her arm, she went into the house. Patsy O'Reilly, giving them another hot look, followed her sister-in-law, head also in the air. They banged the door behind them.

Carl said, "That's the deal, O'Reilly. Thanks for the beer."

"Thanks from me, too," Shorty said.

"I won't move, men."

The farmer's voice held stubbornness. But his was not the angry flaring stubbornness of his wife and sister. His was deep and strong and therefore more dangerous.

"Sorry," Carl said.

He and Shorty mounted and rode out of the clearing without another word, horses kicking up dust as they hit a trail lope.

They rode for a distance in silence. Shorty was the first to speak and his words came slowly from his lips.

"She sure is a awful lovely woman, Carl."

"Patsy or Janet?"

"You know who I mean. Patsy is purty in a way, but she's married — I'm talkin' about Janet, of course."

"Oh forget it."

"She's as purty as Birdie Kalin."

Carl drew Gray Blanket to a halt. "For

Gawd's sake, Shorty, quit talking. We got trouble ahead of us, short man."

"We sure have, boss."

"When word reaches the Bar T about the O'Reillys being on Corporation range, Matthew Kalin will call me in and order me to run them off."

"How will he ever know about these nesters bein' on his range?" Shorty asked, face lightening. "He can never ride a hoss this far. We don't need to tell him, you know."

Carl shook his head slowly.

Shorty asked, "What's wrong with that plan?"

"I draw wages from the Bar T. The Corporation buys the time I spend on this earth. Not to report these nesters would be to work against the iron that boards me, feeds me, pays me wages. And that ain't Hoyle in Carl Hudson's book."

"Ah, throw that book away — and git another, Carl."

Carl rubbed his whiskery jaw. It sounded like a file rubbing against his hand.

Shorty continued with, "Look, they only occupy a small hunk of this range. Not a spit in the ocean. God done give us all plenty of land. No human hog has a right to rob his brother. Besides, them people has filed on their land — which is what *Mister* Matthew

Kalin and them millionaire bankers of his has not did."

"Not a scrap of paper," Carl said.

Shorty spat tobacco juice on a sagebrush. "That beer sure tasted almighty good. Sure would save a man some money to have a woman that could make beer like that. Well, Carl, you're my boss — what you say goes with me, fella, even though I might not like it one bit."

Carl momentarily evaded the issue, something out of the ordinary for him. "We got calves to run out of the brush and brand," he said.

FOUR

For six days Carl Hudson lived and wrestled and fought with his problem. Sometimes he would awaken in the dead of night, when the ranch lay wrapped in dark stillness, and he would think of the O'Reilly clan. He wondered if they had finished their house. He wondered if the women had made any more beer. One day he almost headed out at dawn for the farm on the rim of Wishing Hills. But the schedule called that this day he stay at the Bar T and help brand some colts. Every move he made was regimented and overlooked by that silent devil, the schedule. He wondered if he were interested in the O'Reillys as a clan or if his interest centered more on Janet. He told himself that his interest centered on the clan as a whole because they were so hard-working and hospitable. But, as he told himself this, he knew it was not the absolute truth — Janet had sure looked clean and girlish and wholesome holding that baby. He even forgot temporarily she had also held something else — a Winchester .30-30 rifle.

About sundown on the sixth day, Shorty Madlin came into the blacksmith shop, where

Carl was making himself a knife out of a file.

"I was walkin' past the house," Shorty panted, "when Kalin sticks his fat head out the door, stops me an' tells me to tell you to come to the office on the run, child."

Carl forgot his knife. He stared at Shorty. Shorty had a miserable look in his eyes.

"He sure seemed disturbed," Shorty said. "You don't suppose? Maybe he's heard something we didn't want him to."

"What do you figure, Shorty?"

Shorty shrugged. "Might be; might not be. But me, I'm no hand at solvin' riddles. Mister Kalin said for you to get up there right pronto, Carl." He emphasized the word mister. "Let me know what it is all about, huh?"

"If I live through it," Carl said. "Maybe I should have told him."

Shorty said nothing. His eyes mirrored anguish. Finally he blurted out, "Man, I'm afraid, I am."

Carl looked at the knife in the vise.

"I don't feel so good myself, Shorty."

"He said for you to come on the run," Shorty reminded.

"He can go to hell."

There was a tone of finality about the foreman's words, and Shorty studied him more carefully. Shorty was about fed up with the Corporation and the schedule. He wanted to stick around Birdie, though. He was not fooling himself one bit about Birdie, for she was a rich man's spoiled daughter and he was only a cowhand. When he talked to Carl, he was not serious about Birdie; Carl knew this, so did he — it was something to joke about. And she was nice to look at. When your job calls you miles away from the closest woman for months at a time, just to look at a woman — be she fat or skinny, ugly or beautiful — was something nice and good.

"None of our riders has rid over in the Wishin' Hills," Shorty said.

Carl took the knife from the vise. He had already made a sheath out of buffalo hide and he crammed the knife in this and hung it on the wall. Then he washed his hands in the water bucket. He seemed to be in no hurry and seemingly had not a care in the world.

Squinting in the soot-streaked piece of mirror on the wall, he asked a question: Was Birdie also in the office?

"Yes. Why?"

Carl smiled. "Gotta look my purtiest for her. Might beat your time."

"That sure wouldn't be hard to do," Shorty moaned.

Carl had his hair combed to his satisfaction. He straightened, tugging down on his shirt, said, "Well, here goes nothing. Catch me when I get throwed out."

"In my arms?"

Carl grinned and shook his head. "If it is what I think it is going to be, I'll come out in small pieces — so get the washtub from the bunkhouse."

"Let's hope it ain't that."

Carl walked leisurely up the gravel walk. He knew that behind the thick drape he was being watched by Matthew Kalin. He looked lazy and contented, merely a man going to pay a social call, but inside his heart jumped and wobbled, and he had his full measure of misgivings. He reached the end of the walk and climbed the three steps onto the porch.

As usual, to make Kalin mad, he entered without knocking, despite the sign on the door that said, *Knock first, and come in only if invited.* A rule of the Corporation. The interior of the house was darker than the outside but the features of Kalin and his daughter could be seen clearly.

Carl nodded at Birdie, who nodded back, and then he said, "Shorty came runnin' into the blacksmith shop and said you wanted to see me, Kalin." He deliberately left off the *Mister.*

Matthew Kalin was seated at his desk, sagging back in the swivel chair, a pencil between thumb and forefinger, and his daughter stood behind him. His eyes on Carl, the millionaire spoke to his daughter, and Carl noticed the surly edge to his domineering voice.

"Girl, sit down and keep your mouth closed, please."

Birdie got red-faced, but she said nothing — she merely stuck out her tongue at him, then winked at Carl. She remained standing close to the wall.

Matthew Kalin did not invite Carl to sit down although there were two vacant chairs to Carl's right.

"Carl, I have here a letter — it just came from town with the mail — and it is from the owner of the Circle R ranch, and he writes me from Sulphur Springs. The mail is so poor it took four days to be delivered to Willow Bend. But that is neither here nor there. I do not know the owner of the Circle R, but this letter brings me a bit of startling information."

"Oh?"

"Nesters have moved in on our Bar T grass, Hudson."

Carl said, "Nesters?"

"Yes, nesters. Farmers. Sodbusters. Pumpkin rollers. Call them what you want, but they are in our grass — so this letter reports."

"Where are they located?" Carl asked.

Matthew Kalin got laboriously to his feet

60

and trod across the room to the big wall map that showed the outlines of the Bar T and other Wyoming ranches. He carried the letter with him.

"According to this letter these farmers have located on a creek over on the edge of the Wishing Hills." His gaze roamed to the map and a pudgy forefinger moved along Wishing Creek until it found the approximate location of the O'Reilly farm, and there the finger stopped and tried to punch a hole in the map, but the wall backed up the map and made this impossible.

"Right there, Hudson."

"What's the name of the nester?" Carl asked.

Again, the eyes stabbed the letter. "Name of Reilly. Oh, hell, no — O'Reilly, not Reilly. A husband, a wife, a baby — and some other woman."

"Only one family has moved in, I take it?" he asked.

"Only one."

Matthew Kalin's eyes were on Carl Hudson now. Carl deliberately moved to make the spur rowels clang. The eyes showed a touch of anger.

The thick lips opened and closed. "These O'Reillys will have to go, Hudson. If we allow one bunch of farmers to stay it will only encourage others to settle, and if this range is not kept intact, the Corporation will lose this ranch to the settlers. The Corporation cannot allow this to happen. Its stockholders look for a profit and a profit cannot be made if we lose our free range. These farmers have to move. Is that clear, Hudson?"

Carl merely nodded. He did not trust himself to speak. He glanced at Birdie Kalin. She might have been one of the Corporation's biggest stockholders, for her face was very serious. Carl had never seen her so serious before. The hardness of her father's deep voice had made her very solemn. Carl got the impression that when Matthew Kalin really got mad the fur really flew and Birdie knew this from past experience. And her eyes were deadpan and solemn as she watched him.

Birdie broke the silence. "What are we going to do about these farmers, Father?"

Matthew Kalin said surlily, "We want no words from you, girl," and he looked up at Carl. "There is one thing about this problem I find hard to understand, Hudson."

Outside a bronc neighed down in the corral. Carl asked, "And that?"

"You and Shorty Madlin spent some days running strays out of the Wishing Hills. According to this letter, at that date these farmers had already settled in the Hills. Yet you never ran across their farm, nor did you mention seeing their farm to me."

Carl had had enough. He hated to lose his job — the thought of that extra twenty per month was a devilish thought — but a man, he realized, had to retain his self respect. He had done a lot of thinking. By the time he had enough money saved he would be about thirty. When you are in your twenties, the thirties constitute old age. He decided to grab the bull by the tail.

"Shorty an' me found their farm," he said.

The heavy head jerked. Disbelief and doubt touched the pale eyes and then fled before the onrush of controlled anger.

"You two — what?"

Well, I surprised the old boy, Carl told himself. Sure good to see him surprised, he prides himself on his self control. He took three paces to the window, making his spurs chime and then he turned.

"Yes, they were located there, when Shorty and I rode the Wishing Hills for them mavericks. They were located on Wishing Crick — the farmers, not the cattle, I mean. Nice family."

"So you knew this all the time! Then why didn't you report this fact to me the minute you rode into this yard?"

Carl shrugged. "I thought it would be of no use."

"No use!" Matthew Kalin almost shuddered. "What gave you such a stupid damned thought, Hudson?"

"Shorty and me talked to them. We warned them. We told them that the policy of the Bar T stockholders would not allow farmers to settle on Bar T range. We figured that information would scare them into movin'."

"And you never followed up that threat?"

Carl knew what the millionaire meant, but he played dumb.

"I don't foller you a foot," he said.

"Are you stupid, man? What I mean is this: You never at any time rode back to their homestead site to see if they had left?"

Carl heard a noise to his right and he turned rather rapidly, for his nerves were not too steady. Then vigilance ran out of his lanky body as he recognized the man who had slid in from the side room, moving back the heavy drapes used as a door. Carl did not like this man. His name was Winn Carter. He had come west with Matthew Kalin. He was a bony and ugly man about six feet tall and Carl judged him to be about forty years of age, but the craggy face was hard to fit into a chronological bracket. Carter had a rough, hawked nose and his eyes were without color — they seemed to look right through a man. He was Kalin's bodyguard. Back East he had probably toted his sidearm in a holster under his shoulder. But here on the range he packed two guns, each tied down low. And Carl knew that Winn Carter knew how to use those two bone-handled .45s tied to his flat thighs. Carl had seen him draw.

Winn Carter said nothing. His lifeless eyes looked at Carl with what seemed faint amusement, and this utter lack of personal regard almost made Carl say something hot, but he held his temper in time.

Carl hated him for what he was — a cold-blooded man hired by a millionaire's money, a hired killer. Between them had been intense dislike, and both were aware of this despite the fact neither had mentioned it. The other hands hated the lanky killer, too. Winn Carter did not associate with the other Bar T riders. He kept to himself. He lived in the main house with Kalin. He seldom spoke and when he did it was to say something derogatory. Now he nodded, said nothing, and moved back against the wall, standing there watching with his back to the wall. Watching, saying nothing, just looking.

Carl knew the gunman had been secreted in the next room. He had heard them talking and had come out to back up his boss.

"Why didn't you ride back?" the millionaire demanded. "That was your job, Hudson. Why didn't you check back?"

Carl shrugged. He was calm now. "I told you once. I thought they would move. I told them about the Corporation being so powerful." Did his voice sound too cynical, or not enough? "But I guess they thought we were joking."

Matthew Kalin looked past Carl. He was in deep thought momentarily. Carl knew his place: he was but a checker on the board and soon Kalin would move him. If he clung to the board, Kalin would get another checker to move. A number of hands on the Bar T wanted Carl's job. Carl knew that; Kalin knew it; Birdie was aware of it; Winn Carter knew it, too — and Carter did not care. Carl glanced at Carter. Their eyes met, held: Carter's eyes held no life. Carl thought, *Hell, I'm no better than he is, 'cause I spend Corporation money, too*. That thought was disgusting. Was any job worth this treatment?

"What is your plan, Hudson?"

"I only work here, Kalin. I carry out orders. You're the boss."

Maybe his anger showed in his voice. For Winn Carter lifted his gaunt shaggy head and stabbed him a glance before lowering his eyes again. Birdie opened her mouth, her tongue

66

touched her bottom lip, and then she slowly closed her mouth. But Matthew Kalin did not look at Carl.

"You take a man and ride over there tomorrow, Hudson. Give them final orders to move — say, twenty-four hours. No, make it two days — forty-eight hours. Then, inside of that time limit, you check again, understand?"

Carl nodded. "And if they are still on their homestead — what then?"

"We'll run them out with flame and guns," the millionaire said, clipping his words. "We'll make an example of them. Our Corporation is powerful and has high-priced lawyers. The local law won't dare arrest one of the Corporation's men. We pay most of the taxes in this country. I can get the sheriff out of office if he crosses me. Even if we have to kill them, they have to go."

"Kill — even the women?" Carl asked.

Winn Carter answered, "Yes, the females."

Carl turned on him. They eyed each other. "I never asked you," Carl pointed out. "I asked Kalin."

Carter said nothing. Hate glistened then in his eyes, making them oblique and deadly. Then the thin lips smiled but the smile was forced and the hate turned to blue steel.

"Don't fly off the handle with me, cowpuncher."

Kalin turned in the chair. "That's enough of that talk, Winn."

Carter swung his eyes to his boss. Then he murmured, "You're the boss."

Carl went outside.

He breathed deeply. Out here the air tasted better and cleaner. He lived in the foreman's shack — a log building set just west of the bunkhouse — and he sat down on the bench in the shade. After a few minutes Shorty Madlin came bow-legging around and he sat down beside Carl.

"Well, boss?"

"We were right," Carl said. "We had a set-to. I did some talking and he did some. I damned near bounced my job in his fat jowls."

"Winn Carter listening, like usual?"

"He was there. We had some words, too. Birdie was there. Her father told her to shut up, and by golly she shut up."

"Well, I'll be danged."

"Tomorrow I'm supposed to take a man and ride over to the Wishing Hills and tell the O'Reillys they got two days — just forty eight hours — to slope out-a the country, abandon their homestead. The owner of the Circle R took it upon his old shoulders to write to Big Money. The letter was slow in comin' to Wil-

68

low Bend — has to go all the way to Cody, you know, and then back. But the O'Reillys have to leave."

"What if they refuse to jerk stakes?"

"Fire," Carl said. "And lead."

Shorty's brows rose. "You mean that fat devil would order us men out to burn them down and kill them — kill them two women an' that little baby?"

"So he said. Corporation lawyers would pertect the outfit, he said. It would never get into court, he claimed. He's as cold-blooded as a clam in frozen mud."

"Well, I'll be — the dirty old . . ."

"Swear louder," Carl said, "so he can hear."

Shorty got to his feet. "I'm shoeing that danged pack mule, so I'd best be at work, or Money Bags will can me. Time was when we had a blacksmith to do the shoeing. How come he got the can?"

Carl grinned. "Save money. Cut a man off the payroll. Each man has to shoe his own stock now. Save the Corporation money. Make a bigger dividend this next spring. So long, sweetheart."

"I'm goin' ride over to Wishin' Crick with you tomorrow, huh?"

"I'll think it over."

"Why don't you take Mike Hendricks?"

Carl had to smile. "You want Mike out of

the way so you can have a clear field with Birdie, huh? Man, you have slipped your picket-pin; thet girl don't want you. She couldn't even wash dishes or sweep a floor."

"Or milk my cows," Shorty said.

"You talk like a farmer."

Shorty looked down at him and his face was serious. "You might have said somethin' there, Carl. Maybe this having a farm isn't so bad."

Carl watched him.

"I've spent my life in a hard saddle punchin' the other man's cows for wages that would starve a dog to death. I've started work at sunup an' quit at sundown . . . or later. I've slept on the hard ground in rain and snow and in a haymow like a coyote. Curled in the hay. I've been treated like most people don't treat their dogs."

Carl smiled. But his smile held no mirth. Every word the little cowpuncher said rang true.

"You sound wound up, Shorty."

"I am. I've rid hosses until I got calluses on my seat. I got no money. Maybe it would be better if the calluses were on my paws from hangin' onto a plow? Or from milkin' a cow — *my own cow*, though?"

And Shorty ambled across the hoof-packed dusty compound, heading for the mule that stood in front of the blacksmith shop, tied to the hitching post there. Carl went into a deep study. He had work to do. He did not intend to do this work. He felt punk. He kept thinking of Janet. And the baby. And Patsy, too — and John. A cold beer, bottled and put in the spring to keep cool. He heard boots coming and looked up and saw Birdie Kalin.

"May I sit down, Carl?"

"Your father owns the bench," Carl grumbled. "You'll inherit it when he croaks. But if you've come to pick on me, take your axe over and whack Shorty or Mike to death. They'll like it — I won't."

"Carl, such language."

She sat down beside him. She rustled and she smelled nice. Women fought by underhanded methods, and some of their methods came in bottles — either alcohol or perfume. She slid over and her hand went over one of his.

"Sometimes Daddy talks awful rough and he doesn't mean to be rough. He's a nice man, inside."

Carl almost replied, "Maybe he is to you — but he's never shown a soft streak to me," but he held his words in time. After all, Money Bags *was* her father. So he said, "When he feels like getting real rough, honey, just have

71

him jump at a gent named Carl Hudson, will you?"

Her deep eyes were on him. She had the habit of watching a man's face closely, eyes appraising him. She did this now. Carl looked across space at the mule. The mule didn't like Shorty, who was trying to fit a shoe to the off forehoof. The dusk was growing thicker. Overhead a nighthawk swooped down, winds braking his flight, making a zooming sound. He snagged a bug and sailed on over the windmill. Carl looked at the girl.

They looked at each other for a long moment.

Carl felt his blood quicken, and he was the first to look away — a fact which gave her some satisfaction, he guessed.

"Play along with Dad, Carl."

"Why?"

"He can make you — or break you."

He said, "What difference would it make to you?"

He had her there. She didn't want to make any commitments. She wanted to play just so far, to the edge of danger, and then pull back into her own class, her own kind. This she did now. She did it gracefully, for she had had much practice, and she pouted like a girl who just had her braids tipped with ink in an inkwell.

"I can't understand you Western men."

"I don't sell," Carl said. "I don't scare, either, or at least I think I don't." He pushed her hand off his, the gesture almost rough.

"Carl!"

"Goodbye."

"I'm not leaving."

"Goodbye."

"My father owns this ranch. When it passes to me I'm going to fire you." She laughed shakily. "You're the first man I have ever thrown myself at. And you treat me like I was a dog."

Carl glanced around. The dusk was very thick. Shorty was leading the mule toward the barn. No other Bar T men were in the vicinity. They were washing up for evening chuck. Carl thought, What the hell?, and he put his right arm around her narrow waist. He did not have to pull her close. She came close of her own accord, her full thigh pressing against his hip. She was near and warm and firm and the perfume added its gentle aura. Her golden hair was tumbling back, her head was raised, her eyes were closed, her lips opened slightly.

She clung to him, putting the emphasis on the right spots. Finally they broke and Carl thought, She's kissed plenty of them — she knows how.

Her eyes were dreamy. "I loved that," she whispered.

Carl grinned. "Thanks for the buggy ride. It would be no dice all the way through. You just want to play so far, no further. I'll be out in the saddle at daybreak. I'm an old man. Good night, again — and for the last time."

"Good night!"

He watched her walk away, back straight. He should have felt good and he should have grinned. He had just kissed a million dollars.

And it wasn't every day a man got to kiss that much money.

FIVE

For some reason Carl Hudson slept very little that night. He tossed and turned, had a million thoughts, and when sleep came, it came toward morning. Dawn seeped in through the windows and he got out of bed and grumbled and stretched and he was still tired. He washed outside in the big washbowl and then he shaved. He hated shaving but since the Corporation had taken over the Bar T, a ruling had been posted that each man had to shave at least every two days. No other ranch would have dared pass such a law. But jobs were scarce, what with the Eastern money panic, so the cow-punchers had to shave — or starve looking for a new job.

His straight-edged razor scraped and Carl thought. He wouldn't take Shorty along to Wishing Creek. Nor would he take Mike Hendricks, either. He'd go alone. His shaving chore through he went to the mess shack, where he ate his usual stack of hotcakes — and had four strips of bacon, some coffee and some biscuits. After smoking a cigarette, he was ready to leave. He did not give orders direct to his men while they ate, as he used to do when the Old Man had owned the Bar T. Now, once a week, he left orders with Kalin, writing down the chores each hand was to do each day, and Kalin in turn had his daughter post them on a big bulletin board, there on the side of the barn.

The hands were gathered around the bulletin board, most of them cursing their jobs, when he came to the barn, but he paid nobody any attention — his mood was anything but light.

"Somebody steal your best wife?" Mike Hendricks joked.

Carl said nothing.

Shorty asked, "Am I ridin' with you, boss?"

"Ridin' alone."

"Ah, Carl . . ."

"You heard me. You got chores to do. Do them."

Shorty said no more. He led out his sorrel and saddled him outside. Carl had his gear on the saddlerack by the door. He got the bit in Gray Blanket's jaws and led his mount outside.

He stopped and looked at Birdie Kalin.

She was astraddle her pinto, her silver-inlaid saddle reflecting the early sunlight. Her pinto tossed his head, rolling the cricket in his bit. The sound was sharp and shrill. She was a rich man's daughter and she was beautiful, but Carl was grumpy, although his heart did miss a beat or two.

"Where are you goin'?" he demanded.

"To Wishing Creek. With you, Carl."

He shook his head. "Did the old boy okay it?"

"Quit calling my father the *old boy*. On Wall Street they see him coming and they jump up and salute."

"This isn't Wall Street. Did he say you could come?"

"Never asked him."

"You ride up to the house and ask him."

"He is still in bed."

"Go up and wake him up and ask him."

"Sure," she said cynically, "sure. And where will the great Carl Hudson be, while I'm out of sight in the house? He'll be beating away from here hell for leather and I never can find him in the badlands."

Carl had to smile. "You stay home."

"I won't."

"You do as I say."

She leaned forward on her stirrups and her voice was level. "Listen to me, Mr. Hudson. You might be range-boss of this spread, understand? But you aren't my boss. My father owns this outfit. If the outfit makes enough money he'll keep it — and if he keeps it, someday it'll be mine. So don't try to boss

Birdie Kalin around."

"I'm not riding with you — alone."

"Afraid I might take advantage of you?"

"I'm not going to have tongues wag about us, Birdie. Shorty is going with us."

"Chaperone?"

"Yes, you could call him that. Oh Shorty!"

"The little devil," she murmured. "I hate him."

Shorty came up, leading his horse. He said, "Well, Miss Birdie," and his hat came off to sweep almost to his knees. "What's on the great mind, boss?"

"You ride with us, Shorty."

"With us?"

"Yes, us."

Shorty went into saddle without using his stirrup. "Let's ride, then," he said. "Come on, Birdie."

They loped out of the yard, dust puffing behind them. Shorty took the lead and Birdie rode close to Carl.

"Damn you," she hissed.

"You must love me."

"Why do you say that?"

"You swear at me."

"I could — beat you!"

"What with?"

"A club."

"I'll cut one for you when we get to the

crick," Carl Hudson said, and grinned.

Carl figured they would reach the O'Reilly farm about noon. The distance to Wishing Creek and back was a good day's ride in the heat. They would change horses at the other end of the line for the Bar T had a pasture on upper Wishing Creek and they kept saddlehorses there. He wished he had been riding alone. He had wanted to talk to the O'Reillys without having any other Bar T people along.

Carl said little if anything. Birdie talked to Shorty who smiled like a dog getting his coat brushed. They chatted and Carl thought. This was a hell of a thing to do, he realized.

"A nickel for your thoughts?" Birdie once asked.

Carl grunted, "Since the war things are higher. Used to be a penny."

"For you, a nickel."

"For me, no thoughts."

"Mind a blank, eh?"

"Total blank."

By eleven they were riding down on the Wishing Creek bottom. They watered their horses and then rode toward the O'Reilly farm. John O'Reilly was plowing. The ground was hard. It had been some time since the last rain, but his plow managed to dig some sort of furrow — he had four horses hitched abreast, one walking in the furrow and one in the plowed area. He saw them coming and pulled in, the horses letting their tugs go slack, their flanks rising and falling, sweat rimming their collar pads and around their blinders.

Carl found himself thinking that if he had four horses on a plow he would run one team ahead of the other and no horse would walk in the plowed ground, but two horses would walk in the furrows. This way horse power would be conserved, for the plowed area made for hard walking.

They were about a hundred yards from the new house. Carl noticed that the roof was in place, and from where he was it looked like the two women were putting in the windows. Chickens clucked in the yard, the cows grazed along the creek, and the entire farm looked peaceful. Carl found himself admiring the little spread.

O'Reilly's eyes held suspicion. Up at the house, the women stopped working and started towards them.

"Howdy, people," the farmer said.

His eyes shuttled from one to the other, then rested on Birdie, who was watching the women come from the house. "I take it this is maybe your wife, Hudson?"

Carl shook his head. "I couldn't pay for the silver on that saddle if I worked all my life.

This is Birdie Kalin, daughter of Matthew Kalin. Matthew Kalin is the head man of the Corporation that bought the Bar T."

"I've heard tell of him."

Carl spoke to the farmer in a low tone of voice. "John, we never rid here for trouble. This is no doin' of mine. But the owner of the Circle R wrote to Kalin and told him about you. He climbed my hide up and down the middle for me an' Shorty not reportin' you people over here on Wishin' Crick."

"So you never told him, eh?"

Shorty substantiated with, "We sure didn't, Mr. O'Reilly."

The farmer's eyes moved from one to the other. "I believe you," he said. "I think you two are right nice guys, but maybe you're not — at that."

"Why do you say that?" Carl asked.

"You work for a skunk outfit. A clean-smelling man would never be around skunk smell. So maybe that makes you skunk, too?"

By this time the women had arrived. They both seemed interested in Birdie. Three women — one mounted; two on foot — studied each other. Between them was that mutual long-born hate women always seem to have for the others of their sex.

Carl said, "You got a good theory, John.

I'm not disputin' it, fellow. Fact is, Shorty an' me been thinkin' along the same lines, and the thought ain't one bit pleasant."

"He's right," Shorty said.

Carl said, "The Big Boss said you could have two days — forty-eight hours from now — to get out."

The farmer looked at Birdie. "By the Big Boss I guess you mean Kalin. This gal's father?"

"The same," Carl said.

The women listened. They watched Birdie. They watched Shorty. They watched Carl. They were tough pioneer women and they knew how to shoot those shotguns and those rifles and they'd fight until they died. Carl looked at Janet. Even in times of stress she was sure pretty. She looked at him but her eyes were not admiring and they seem to say, you low-lived devil. Carl did not feel too pert about this. Janet and that rifle did not look good together. She looked much better with a baby under her arm. Then Janet looked up at Birdie.

"I saw you once — in Willow Bend. You're Birdie Kalin, ain't you?"

"Miss Kalin," Birdie corrected.

The women eyed each other. They were two cats — one, a registered Persian, the other, a beautiful crossbred. They circled each other. They snarled and spat. They had their claws out.

Patsy spoke to her husband. "We won't leave."

John O'Reilly nodded. "They can't chase us off our land, honey. We got first filing papers on it and everything is legal and honest. We'll get the sheriff out to pertect us. We're taxpayers and we'll demand pertection."

"Won't do you folks no good," Shorty said.

Janet studied him. "Why not?"

Birdie Kalin answered. "The sheriff is a friend of the Bar T, girl. The sheriff is an old cowman. The Bar T is a cow outfit. Old cowmen don't like farmers. The Bar T pays an enormous amount of taxes — taxes pay the sheriff's salary. The sheriff will close his eyes, girl."

"Don't girl me, you hussy."

"Don't hussy me, you sodbuster."

Janet said, "Get off that horse and call me that!"

Carl felt like this was getting out of hand.

"For God's sake, women, shut up! This is no time to fight. Birdie, you keep your big mouth shut, understand?"

"Make her shut up, then."

"I'll keep Janet quiet," her brother said. He appealed to his flaming sister. "We got to talk this over, honey. Please."

"Oh — all right." But then anger surged back again. "Oh, what is the use? I'd just be wasting my breath, but I'm going to let go." She did not let go on Birdie. She let go on Carl Hudson. Her eyes glistened with hot anger. She tossed her head angrily. "You are indeed in *good* company, Mr. Hudson. Maybe my brother and his wife might move — to keep their baby from being killed by your rotten cow outfit — but you can be assured Janet O'Reilly will not move, sir. I am returning to the house. My rifle will cover you, though."

Carl was sweating. For a moment, their eyes met, and, before he could say a word, off she stalked.

"Send Matthew Kalin over," the farmer said. "We got to work out a compromise some way. Or I can ride over and see him."

Carl saw his way out. "Do that tomorrow?"

"I sure will."

Patsy spoke in an anxious tone of voice. "Will my husband be — safe, Mr. Hudson?"

Carl nodded. "I personally guarantee his safety. He can ride back with us, if he wants to."

"Be over tomorrow," the farmer said.

"Good enough," Carl said.

"Will the ride do me any good?"

Carl replied truthfully. "I don't know, John."

The Bar T trio rode away, then. They headed toward the pasture on upper Wishing Creek. There they would change horses.

"I sure feel sorry for them people," Shorty said, and then looked quickly at Birdie, hoping he had not said the wrong thing.

Birdie said, "They seem like nice people. I wish I could have seen the baby you told me about, Carl."

Carl looked at her. "You like babies?"

"What woman doesn't?"

They rode in silence. The noon heat was oven thick. It hung to the hills, sucking the little moisture out of the soil, and cattle hung close to cottonwood trees along creeks and waterholes. They would have noon chuck at the pasture.

"I don't like this one bit," Birdie said.

Carl asked, "You don't like *what?*"

"What if they don't move?"

Carl said, "You heard your dad. Flame — and gunfire."

"Oh, that would be terrible!"

"Why not talk to him?"

She looked at him with a smile that was almost cynical. "You are an optimist, Carl. I have no influence over him. Only one inanimate object has ever influenced his life."

Shorty said, "Inanimate? What does that mean?"

"Something that has no life — doesn't run or move or breathe. And that something is round and about two inches in diameter, and it is made of silver and it's got an eagle on one side, I believe, stamped in, and it is called the Dollar — the Almighty Dollar."

"I'd sure hate to be that greedy." Shorty spoke with solemn earnestness.

Birdie said, "Sure, and look at me. College, smart alec dudes, cocktails. No swearee, no cussee, no do this, no do that. Then I come out here and meet you two devils and you treat me like I was a poisoned pup, or something. I make a play for both of you and you get suspicious."

"I'm not," Shorty said hurriedly.

Carl leaned from saddle, put his arm around her slim waist and said, "Honey, I'm sorry," and kissed her. He kissed her for a long, long time — in fact, their ponies pulled them apart. "Now do you feel better?"

"Better? Why, I could walk on water."

"Me, now," Shorty said.

Shorty just had a short, embarrassed peck. Carl grinned and said, "Well, there's the line camp. Birdie, go in and rustle up some chuck, an' me and this long drink of alkali water will round up the horses and shove them into the corral."

"I need help. Let Shorty stay with me."

Shorty's eyes glistened like stars. "Good idea."

Carl said, "Okay, Romeo." They rode through and he shut the gate, still in the saddle. He sort of hated to leave the Bar T. Up to the time the Corporation had brought the spread it had been a pleasant place to work. His ramrod job had been a good job what with that extra twenty bucks per month bonus — it had been good, that is, until Matthew Kalin had hove into view.

He was out here to find out why so many cattle had died in the winter. Carl had told him but the Easterner was dubious. Carl had said they should cut hay. With hay, they could feed cattle in the winter. The snow had been too deep. Cattle did not paw through snow; only horses pawed to feed. The blizzards had been long and the thermometer, at one time, had hit fifty-two below. Carl had told him all these things and he still stayed.

Carl had hoped the fat millionaire would soon pull stakes back for his Eastern mansion, his servants, and Wall Street. But that hope had not yet been fulfilled. He hoped Birdie had not talked her father into staying longer so she could be on the Bar T.

He couldn't understand Birdie.

She had a million bucks. He had nothing except his few hundred in savings, his saddle horses, and his rig. Sometimes she seemed to be making fun of him, trying to add him to her string; other times, like a while back, she had been serious.

He walked to the house. Birdie was frying bacon at the wood stove. She also had a skillet filled with frying spuds. Shorty had a pot of java on the back of the hot stove.

Shorty's face was red from the stove. "She's a good hand with a skillet," he praised. "Jumped right into the job."

Carl sat down at the wooden table. He sent a glance around the line camp. Grub on the shelves, a sack of spuds hanging from the beam so mice could not get into them, and wood in the firebox. The rule was to wash your dishes, and, when you left the camp, have it as clean and spic and span as when you came in. The door was never locked.

Carl remembered the angry eyes of Janet O'Reilly. He put his head in his hands, elbows on the table.

You work for a skunk outfit. A clean-smelling man would never be around skunk smell. So maybe that makes you a skunk, too?

That had really dug into him and hurt.

SIX

John O'Reilly left the Wishing Hills farm at daybreak. He rode an old sorrel gelding and he had an old army saddle on the horse, guiding him with a rope bridle that had a snaffle bit and rope reins. The day turned hot. He should have been home plowing, for soon the soil would be too dry to plow; instead, he was off on a wild goose chase. He wondered if he would really stay if the Bar T moved men against him. He was one man with two women and a defenseless baby. It was good to talk about staying, but when the bullets sang, and the torches lit fire to a man's house . . . He would have to appeal to the sheriff at Sulphur Springs, if his talk with Matthew Kalin failed to bring results. And he had little — if any — faith that this would accomplish anything except sending him on a long hard ride.

The day got hotter and his mind became more uncertain. When he had left Illinois he had heard about trouble from the Indians, but they had not told him about these white Indians called cattle kings. He decided worrying did no good.

He had never been to the Bar T but he

knew where the spread's headquarters was located. The immensity of the outfit surprised him. It was almost like riding into a small town. Cowpunchers were out on riding jobs. There happened to be only one man in sight when he rode into the compound and that man was none other than Carl Hudson. Carl had roped a big bay horse and had thrown him and now the bay was on his side, four legs tied with a length of spotcord rope.

"Howdy, Hudson."

Carl had not heard the farmer ride up behind him.

"Miss my dogs," Carl said.

The farmer studied him. "What was that?"

"We used to have a couple of watchdogs. The Corporation made us get rid of them."

"Like they want to get rid of me, huh?" the farmer showed a lopsided, unhappy smile.

Carl had no answer.

"The Big Boss in the house, Hudson?"

"He's in there — or he was the last I knew, about ten minutes ago. He sent his chore-boy — a gunman named Winn Carter — down to summon me to his office about that time ago. Issued another edict."

"How the hell do you stand it?"

"Maybe I don't."

The farmer grinned uncomfortably. "Reckon I'll go up and beard the Big Bad

Wolf in his den," he said, and turned the old nag toward the hitchrack in front of the long rambling Bar T ranch-house.

John O'Reilly walked across the porch, knocked on the door, and Carl saw that Winn Carter opened the door.

The farmer was not inside more than five or six minutes. Then he came blustering out and crossed the porch and Winn Carter slammed the door behind him. O'Reilly turned his old nag, his boots drummed on the hollow ribs, and the old horse trotted, the farmer riding high on the iron stirrups, his face ashen with anger. He dragged the skate to a halt in front of Carl who looked up from behind the corral.

"The dirty devil. I should have given him two sets of hard knuckles right in his fat gopher face."

"Good you didn't, John. They wanted you to do just that. Then Carter would have had an excuse for shooting you down — protecting his boss."

The farmer caught his temper. "Yes, that killer would have killed me. He watched me like a hawk watches a sparrow. He was waiting for me to make a bad move. Kalin wouldn't even talk to me. Spouted like a bull walrus comin' up among the icebergs. Told me to be out with my family by sundown tomorrow."

"You going to go?"

The farmer had a sane and level gaze now. "I've made up my mind. When I went to that house, I was afraid, but I ain't no longer. There are three of us. We got a rifle, a scattergun, and a pistol. We all three can shoot. Not good, but I could hit Kalin, right in the fat belly, with a rifle ball. Like shooting at a potbellied moose. We fight it out."

Carl felt a touch of alarm. "But John, listen, man. You got two women depending on you. You got that little baby to consider. Kalin will work this slick. He won't tangle with you — not if he can help it. He'll hide behind his money. His money has bought Winn Carter. Carter will ride over alone and pick a fight with you and kill you."

The man had a wooden face.

"Then where will your wife — and Janet — and the baby be?"

"They will have a dead father and husband and brother, but they'll kill Carter — if they get a chance."

"They won't get a chance. Carter will see to that. Man, is any land worth that terrible price?"

"No, the land ain't worth it, Hudson. But I'll tell you something that is worth that price, man. And that is a man's pride."

"Pride is no good after a man is dead."

"No, but it keeps him alive. Without pride, he might just as well be dead. Let me tell you somethin', Hudson, and will you take it in good faith?"

Carl figured he knew what was coming. But he said, "Shoot, man."

John O'Reilly leaned forward, elbows on the fork of his old army saddle. "Now don't get huffy, Hudson. I sort of cotton to you even if you ride on the other side of the fence from me. But I told you that. Janet seems to like you a heap, too. But that is neither here nor there. You don't think pride means anything to a man. I can see why you don't. You have no pride. If you had pride you'd never work for that fat hog in there with his long sour-looking face."

"That all you got to say?"

"Ain't it enough?"

Carl said, "Ride on, farmer."

The farmer turned his old horse and loped away, the heavy hoofs stirring the dust. Carl saw the horse was tired. He would have a hard time covering the twenty odd miles back to Wishing Creek. The farmer, he figured, would walk most of the way, leading the jaded horse. But this was a passing thought; it had no satisfaction. What the farmer had said was no news to Carl. He had, lately, been thinking the same thoughts. He was surprised to hear a voice say, "Heard the conversation, Carl, an' I never did it intentionally — you two never saw me acrost the corral, where I am now."

Carl turned.

Shorty was on the other side of the corral, leaning against the bars. He had a long and very serious look on his face.

"That farmer," said Shorty, "is a brave man, Carl. And what is more, he's a smart man, too."

"Don't talk about it."

"You took it, Carl. So, deep inside, you must admit it is true."

"You draw Kalin money, too."

"And I feel like a whipped puppy. That farmer included all of us in his statement, Carl."

Neither spoke. They watched the farmer reach the brush along the creek. The door to the main house opened. They had expected to see Winn Carter come out looking for Carl. But Birdie Kalin came toward them. She had a tight look on her face. She overlooked Shorty altogether. This did not hurt Shorty too much. He was quick to love, quick to forget. He was already over the peak and coming into the era of forgetfulness.

"Dad sent me down to tell you to come up and see him, Carl."

"Sent you, huh? Since when did he drop Carter for his errand boy and make a messenger out of his daughter?"

"Don't get cynical. Dad knows you and Carter hate each other. He told me to tell you to come on the run. Oh, hello, Shorty."

"Glad you seen me," Shorty said.

She looked at him. "Don't you get sassy with me or I'll spank you over my knee." She looked back at Carl. "The talk with that farmer really upset the old man. After O'Reilly had left the old man took two shots of whiskey. I heard from the next room. They went at it hot and heavy. That farmer upset the old man."

"Good," Carl said.

"He wants you to come right now."

"There's no rush."

"He's real mad."

"Let him get madder."

"He can't get any madder. First time in years I've heard him curse like this. Last time he swore this hard was at a bankers' meeting. He claimed . . ."

"I don't give a damn what he claimed, then or now."

Birdie smiled. "You're hard to get along with, honey. And what is more, your disposition is getting worse each day." She appealed to Shorty. "Shorty, one of the tie-thongs on my saddle's stirrups broke. Help me put a new lace leather in it?"

"Sure thing. What do you aim to do, Carl?"

"Both of you get out of here," Carl said.

They went toward the barn. Carl took the pigging-string off the horse's legs and let him get to his feet. He had no desire to operate for a ringbone or anything else on any horse. He turned the horse into the pasture, opening the corral gate. He was closing the gate when the door of the house opened again.

Carter came down the path, boots grinding on the gravel. He wore boots and a big hat, but he never got on a horse to the best of Carl's knowledge. Carl coiled his rope, covertly watched the gunman approach, and he was tight as a fiddle string inside, his fingers trembling slightly.

Winn Carter had a stormy face.

"Did Birdie come down here and tell you the Big Boss wanted to see you right now, Hudson?"

Carter clipped his words.

"She sure did just that, Carter."

"Then why don't you jump?"

"I'm no jumpin' jack, fellow."

Carter's sunken eyes appraised him.

"Don't joke with me, Hudson. The Big Boss sent me down here to tell you to get to the house — and make pronto tracks."

"I'll get there — when I want to."

Birdie and Shorty had stopped in front of the barn, about three hundred feet away, and they were watching and listening, and Shorty had his hand on his gun, Carl noticed. Evidently Winn Carter saw this, too. He knew that the short cowpuncher and Carl were saddle pals. He turned his eyes on Carl.

Carl said, "Don't sweat, Sonny Boy. Tell his Royal Nibs I'll be right up, after I wash my face, comb my hair, put on a new shirt, and brush my tooth — I only have one left."

"Make it pronto, sabe?"

"I sure will. I'll run my boots down to the ankles getting up to that house. Thanks for coming all this way to let me know my dear boss wants me."

Carl saw the cigarette drop from the thin lip and hit the dust. Then Carter turned and walked back to the house.

Carl grinned. Not a pleasant grin, though.

Carl finished coiling his lasso and he hung it over a corral post and climbed over the corral, leaping to the ground on the opposite side. He walked toward the house, and his nerves were as raw as the back of a saddle-burned horse. He realized he needed this job and needed it bad — he had a small bankroll. Jobs were scarce as hen's teeth, too. But he had made up his mind. He had stood enough. He admired John O'Reilly. O'Reilly, by the same token, did not admire him. The farmer had bluntly told him so.

He stalked in, not knocking. As usual, Matthew Kalin was behind his desk, head down as he read a sheet of paper — which, Carl knew, was just a ruse, to pretend he was busy.

He reminded Carl of a fat bullfrog sitting on a slimy rock.

"You want to see me?" Carl asked.

"That farmer — John O'Reilly — was in here. But you know that — he talked with you at the corral, I noticed. I ordered him to get off our land."

"He told me."

"He has to go, Hudson. Him and his whole damned Irish tribe."

"O Reilly has a deed to his homestead."

"The Bar T was in this country long before O'Reilly settled on Wishing Creek, Hudson. You trying to protect him?"

Winn Carter leaned against the door jamb. Winn Carter seemed lazy, unconcerned; he was a tomcat, and his muscles were long and limber.

"Not particularly."

"The Bar T iron claims squatter's rights to every foot of grass its cattle wander over, Hudson."

"Squatter's rights are no good. The territorial court threw them into the spittoon some months back."

"Are you a lawyer?"

"No . . ." Carl looked at Carter. "But I can read."

Matthew Kalin paused. Evidently, for once, he was stumped. He had expected Carl Hudson to kow-tow to him. Everybody bent a knee to his money. But this man was not bending his knee.

"My job is to hold Bar T range intact for my Corporation. We can't show a profit if we give the grass away. Those farmers have to leave. If they are on their homesteads by the time my edict is up you are to take our men and ride over there and burn down their buildings and run them out of that area."

"That is illegal."

"Don't worry about the legality of it, Hudson. Judges and sheriffs can be bought, you know. There'll be no reprisals from this crude makeshift frontier law."

Carl was not angry — rather, he was disgusted. Disgusted with himself, disgusted with this money-mad man. Kalin moved round the corner of his desk and then stopped and he watched Carl Hudson. Then his fat lips moved.

"Those are my orders, Hudson."

Carl said, "I heard you."

"And you will carry them out, Hudson?"

Carl had made his mind up. He felt a million years younger than when he had walked into this den.

"You can go to hell, Money Bags."

The words snapped and crackled.

Winn Carter moved his shoulder a little, but his eyes and lips showed nothing.

Kalin had stopped as though somebody had put a .30-30 slug through his heart. He seemed like a man who didn't know whether to fall or stand up.

"What — was — that, Hudson?"

"You heard me."

The banker's face was almost purple with blood, his jowls trembling. Now that he had taken the one big step, Carl Hudson felt calm.

"You, Hudson, are discharged."

Carl smiled. "You can't fire me."

"I can't, huh? I hired you. I'll discharge you."

Carl shook his head. "I quit when I came in that door. You never gave me time to hand in my resignation." Two good words — discharge and resignation. He'd rub it in hard.

"You — !"

Carl said, "I'm through, you purple-faced, bogged-down fat toad."

"Don't call me names."

Carl was surprised to see the banker shuffle

forward, fists up. He doubled a fist, hit, and Carl went under the blow. He felt elation tear through him. He knew that the gun of Winn Carter would come into this. Both guns, maybe. Still, he hit Matthew Kalin in the belly. He hit him with a right uppercut. He felt his hard fist smash to the wrist in fat. He heard the man's terrified agonized grunt. Then Kalin went back against the desk. This held him and he gasped, "Carter, earn your money — he hit me — self defense . . ."

Carl said, "Watch those guns, Carter."

Carter was crouched, hands out over his holsters. "I have to pertect my boss."

Carl had his hand on his holstered gun. He could draw and shoot fast, but Winn Carter, he knew, was faster.

They eyed each other.

Kalin had his breath, now. He stood with his back to the desk, out of line of fire. He rubbed his jowls. Carl thought he saw something else beside anger in the millionaire now. Could it be surprise?

Carl knew that the millionaire was not hurt physically. His belly would be sore for a day or two. His pride had been hurt. The Mint had been robbed. A man had hit Mister Matthew Kalin. A cowpuncher — a dumb, stupid, broke cowpuncher — had almost dumped Mister Matthew Kalin on the floor.

101

And with one blow, too.

Carl now knew fear. He was facing two men — one was a noted gunman, swift with either gun, or both. Kalin also might come up with a weapon out of somewhere on his person. Carl wondered if he would get out of here alive. His anger had overjumped his logic. But then hope speared through him. Behind Winn Carter was a window that was open. Through this window had come the barrel of a rifle. Behind the rifle was a heavy face and a finger was around the trigger, and the hammer was back.

Good old Shorty!

Neither Winn Carter or Matthew Kalin had seen Shorty. Now his voice cut through the tension of the room.

"There's a rifle on your back, Carter. That goes for you, too, Money Bags. Just forget about them tin pistols, Mr. Boston Killer. Put your hands up high — good boy, you listen good and can obey orders. Kalin, if you pack hardware, forget you own it."

Kalin had turned, eyes wide. He stared at Shorty. But Winn Carter did not turn. Carter's thin lips moved.

"Madlin," Carter murmured. "Shorty Madlin."

"This Winchester has a hair trigger," Shorty growled. "My finger is trembling to let the trigger go, men. I got the rifle right on your big pot belly, Money Bags."

"You," stormed Matthew Kalin, "are also discharged."

"Not me. I quit this morning. Just forgot to hand in my written resignation. Carl, make it out the back door. I got two saddle hosses outside the door. You put your rifle on the door — leave it open — and I'll come around and mount. Gray Blanket is waitin', fellow."

Carl had his gun out. "You two walk out ahead of me," he ordered.

When Carter walked past him, Carl took the man's two guns, and Carter cursed him with one word, and then his lips went shut. He walked out on the porch. Carl ran his hands over Kalin's bulk, found a shoulder holster, and he threw the gun in the corner, where he had also thrown the guns of Carter.

"Get out on that porch."

By this time, Shorty had come in behind them. Carl got on Gray Blanket and held his rifle on the pair while Shorty mounted, rifle in hand.

"He owes us some wages," Shorty said.

Carl grinned. "Forget it, son."

"We're leavin' our gear behind," Shorty panted.

"Forget that too — for now. Turn your horse and ride to the edge of the barn, next to the brush. Give me a yell when you get there and are ready. Put your rifle on this pair while I ride over to you. My back will be toward them."

"Not a damned hand on the place to stop this," the millionaire mourned.

Winn Carter said, "Doubt if one would take sides even if there was a man on the grounds."

Shorty's yell cut the air. Carl said, "Goodby, *Mister* Kalin," and he looked at Winn Carter and said, "I reckon we'll meet again, Carter."

"I think so."

Kalin said angrily, "Get the hell off this ranch, Hudson. And what is more — stay off it, savvy?"

"With pleasure, *Boss.*"

Carl loped to where Shorty sat his bronc with his rifle on the two men who stood on the porch. Shorty had a crooked, satisfied smile. Birdie came out of the barn. She looked at Shorty's rifle. She saw her father and the gunman standing on the porch, hands shoulder high.

"What in the name of . . . ? You and Shorty playing cops and robbers, Carl?"

"Not cops and robbers," Carl grimly corrected. "Cattle kings and cowboys is the name of this game."

Her eyes were pulled. "You and the old man had a fight — Hey, where are you going?"

He and Shorty had turned their horses sharply, hoofs kicking back dust. One jump or two, and the broncs were roaring down the wagon road, and the high timber and brush, growing along the creek, came in and hid them from the men on the porch, and took them from Birdie's view, also.

Never, in his wildest dreams, had Carl Hudson ever imagined he would leave the Bar T in this manner, his horse running wildly, his boss still panting from the hard fist that had whammed him in the belly.

He was leaving everything he owned in his foreman shack. But it was not much — right now it consisted mostly of dirty clothes, some worn rather thin. He had had no money in the shack; he either deposited his money in the bank, or carried a paycheck or so on his person. His private saddlehorses — horses he owned — were on open range, and he could get them whenever he wanted to. He pulled down his horse and looked at Shorty.

Shorty looked at him.

Both smiled like a couple of happy schoolboys.

"They won't follow us," Carl said. "Mister Matthew Kalin won't want to soil his fat bottom by the seat of a saddle. Carter will nurse his grudge — and wait. And Birdie don't want to see you so bad she will trail you."

105

Shorty chuckled.

They pulled their horses to a gradual halt. Dust boiled behind them, then fanned out, hung on the motionless air, then settled down.

"Where to?" Shorty asked.

"O'Reilly farm, I guess. As good as any place, ain't it?"

"Good as any — right now."

Carl moved his weight on one stirrup, the ugly scene that had taken place fading slowly from his mind.

"You sure saved my bacon from being burned, son. That fire was kind of hot. I lost my perspective, as the fellow says. Man, it sure was good to bury a fist in that tub of suet."

"I never saw that. I got there just as Kalin went back against the desk. Winn Carter was ready for some gunplay when I horned in."

"He's on the payroll, you know."

"Something which we ain't."

"They'd have burned me down between them, Shorty."

Shorty Madlin spoke with mock sincerity. "I went through a great and deep mental struggle before acting, Carl. I looked at Birdie and her loveliness. I thought of your homely stupid-looking mug. I was sick inside like them writer-fellas say when a woman sees her husband gut-shoot her best man-friend. But your homely face won — and don't ask me why, either."

"Somebody once wrote that friendship between two men was stronger than love for a woman," Carl reminded, smiling widely.

"Well, I looks at Birdie and she looks at me — an' them eyes would melt pig iron, they would. Then I thinks like this, 'Shorty Madlin, you ain't jes' a fool — you're an idiot. This heifer don't cotton to you. She's in love with Birdie Kalin.' So I gets my trusty little rifle and makes a visit to the big house and she never even seen me leave the barn."

"I owe you a lot, Shorty."

"Not near as much as I owe you, Carl."

"I don't savvy what you mean."

"You got me away from the Bar T. I never have liked the spread since the Corporation took over. Neither have you, for that matter. We both should have quit months back. But I'm brainless and sometimes I think you got even less brain matter, if any at all."

"Thanks, friend."

"The compliment was well earned, Carl. What we goin' do at that O'Reilly homestead? Look at Janet and sigh an' do some wishin'?"

"We ride right past the spread, Shorty."

"We do, huh? Thanks, father. Where do

we ride for when we ride past the O'Reilly farm?"

"Sulphur Springs."

Shorty looked at him. He knew what Carl Hudson had in mind. Shorty Madlin's eyes glowed. He seemed very, very happy.

"Suits me fine," he chortled.

SEVEN

The County Surveyor was a young man, only twenty-one. And here he was, in a county office, the boss of it, too.

He looked at the two cowpunchers who had come to his long counter and he thought, Lord, they're crummy-looking men, and he decided not to get too close to them, for they might have lice.

"Something, cowboys?"

"Two homestead entry blanks," Carl Hudson said.

The surveyor looked at them again. Anybody who wanted to take up a homestead, in his opinion, was crazy.

"Don't you two cowpunchers work for the Bar T?" he asked.

"We usta," Shorty Madlin said. "But no longer. We want to file on two homesteads, like my pard here just said."

"You are the first two cowboys who ever came in here wanting to make homestead entries. Have you got your homesteads staked out?"

"We got the rough outlines staked out," Carl Hudson said. "We want you to run the finished lines, after we make our homestead entries and pay our filin' fees. You're federal land agent too, for this area, we understand."

"One of my many duties," the young man said, bursting with importance. He turned to his desk. "I have some forms here somewhere."

He rummaged through loose papers on his desk. Carl looked around the office at the bound volumes of records and felt the closed-in feeling that a man of the saddle has in front of a desk or within four walls. He and Shorty had spent a day marking out the rough outlines of two homesteads.

They had decided to stake out their farms close to the farm of the O'Reilly clan. They had cut tall willow posts along the creek and had used these as corner posts, sighting from the boundaries of the O'Reilly place.

Shorty had looked over the homesteads. "Sure nice pieces of land. First, good sandy loam — raise good crops. Crick runs through them for water. We could dam the crick up above and run ditches out along the hills and irrigate, too, Carl."

"I've thought of that."

"We can raise some stock, too. Run the cows back in the bresh in the rough kentry. I wish we had our shacks built."

"Wish in the Wishing Hills, huh?"

"We gotta build two shacks. Janet looks at you and her eyes get mooney and soft."

"Be a good idea, anyway," Carl had said. "One log house on your property, one on mine. But we could share the barn together — for a spell, anyhow."

"Right. Wish Janet had a sister."

"She has got one."

"But Patsy is married."

"We'd better get to town. Been about a day since Kalin and Carter run us off. Tonight is the night, ain't it, for Kalin to hit at the O'Reilly's?"

"Should be tonight. He might not hit, though."

"We'd better get to town and back. We got to help them. Us farmers got to stick together. Remember the story about the man with a bunch of sons what fought all the time and how the man got some sticks and he couldn't break the sticks when they was in a bunch — but when he got one alone, it busted easy."

"Almost forgot that," Shorty said. "Fourth reader. I went to the fifth. How many readers did you go through?"

"Not enough."

Both had been joking, apparently without a worry in the world, but both had been tense, underneath.

Now they stood in front of the young surveyor. He had placed a map on the counter and had unfolded it. He looked at it like he was the only man in the world who could read it.

Although to him the map was upside down, Carl could read it immediately.

"Where are these two homesteads?" the county surveyor asked.

Carl's long index finger pinpointed the Hills. "Right there," he said.

The surveyor looked and scowled.

"I haven't had time to survey that land yet."

"The gover'ment has surveyed it," Carl said.

The surveyor looked up. "How do you know?"

"We found the section line markers. Concrete, they are. We also found the meridian markers made by the gover'ment surveyors."

"Oh yes, that is right."

"Didn't you survey the boundaries of the O'Reilly farm?" Shorty asked in child-like innocence.

"Yes, I did."

"Well," said Carl, "our homesteads almost border the O'Reilly farm. Like I said, we used O'Reilly's corner post for a line to shoot a border from."

"Your homesteads are on grazing land claimed by the Bar T," the young man said.

"The Corporation won't let you settle there."

Carl almost winced. *Corporation,* again . . . "We'll chance that," he said. "Make out our filing papers and put the best description of the land in it you can, for now."

"You won't be there long."

"That's our lookout, mister," Carl said.

The man did not like the tone of the tall cowpuncher's voice. Best thing to do was get rid of them — put them on Bar T land. They had asked for it. So he scribbled out the entries, got his filing fees, and had the pair sign the entries, and then he gave them their duplicates.

"All set until you make final papers, men. You two are farmers now, not cowhands. And good luck to both of you."

"Same to you, surveyor."

Shorty and Carl went outside. The sun was blistering hot.

Shorty spoke in a doleful voice. "Already my little hands have calluses from holding a lurching, bucking plow in a furrow. Where to now, partner?"

"We need some farmin' equipment."

"You pick it out. What I know about this could be wrut on the head of a pin. And not a hatpin either. To think that Mrs. Madlin's shortest son would fall so low in the social scale as to become a pun'kin roller. There's

113

a lot I don't know about this farmin'. Born on a farm in Ioway but left there when a button, so learned nothing about it. But right off the bat I'd say we needed a wagon to haul things in, like grub and equipment — small equipment, that is — and we need some bobwire, too. Bobwire would be first, huh?"

"Yes, and we need a team."

"Hell, yes, we do. We can make workhosses out of Gray Blanket and my horse, but we need more than one team for heavy work like plowing. We can harness break your other horses, too, and that will give us enough horses to run two work rigs out — like my plowin' with four horses an' you discin' with four behind me."

"I'll go to the hardware store. You find yourself a cup of java."

"You got all your money. I ain't got much."

"They know me at the hardware store. I can write a check on my money in the Willow Bend bank."

Down on the railroad siding, a locomotive wheezed. Farmers walked up and down Main Street and teams and rigs — spring wagons, wagons, buggies, buckboards — were at the tie-poles and hitchracks. Merchants were making more money because there were more people now that the farmers had moved in.

"Takes people to make trade," Shorty said,

when they met up again.

They had already discussed finances. They would go fifty-fifty on everything. By combining their farms they would need just one-half the machinery they would use if each farmed independently of the other.

"I heard some farmers talkin' over their coffee, Carl. Seems as if a few days ago the Circle R got its punchers and rode out against some farmers but the farmers had done organized and they had a few shots atween them but the sheriff and his deputies sailed in."

"What happened then?"

"Some of the Circle R waddies are still in the local calaboose. The whole spread is under a peace bond — a big one too — includin' the owner."

"Oh," Carl said, brows rising. "So — the sheriff rides a straight fence, huh? That means then that the local Law has finally turned against King Cow, I'd say. How far out were these farmers located from town?"

"Only a few miles. And there is the catch. Our spread is way out — fifteen miles or so, must be."

"About that."

"And there ain't but three of us men, which don't make up a very big army, and we don't control many votes, then. These other farmers numbered a dozen, so I guessed."

115

"We never have no luck," Carl said.

They completed their inquisitive tour of the town and went back to dicker with the hardware store owner. He had shipped in a lot full of farming equipment — he was making money hand over fist, too. He was exuberant with success and money. He had discs and harrows and wagons and buggies and plows — both disc and mold-board — on the lot. They bought a disc plow and some harnesses and a wagon. The price of the wagon seemed very high, and Carl remarked about this fact to the hardware man.

"Take it or leave it, Hudson. If you don't buy it, somebody else will — and at my price. Truck wagon, steel wheels, oak reach. Best wagon made — handle nothing but the best."

Carl gave in. "All right."

They also bought a team of workhorses from the local horse-dealer. They knew more about horses than they did about wagons. This was a team of matched gray Percheron geldings that had good blood. They looked at their teeth — the horses were about five-year-olds — and they looked at the horses' legs. They paid a hundred dollars for the team and got some collar pads thrown in. By this time noon had come. They ate at the Silver Spur and Shorty promptly fell in love with the waitress, who paid him no attention.

116

"We'd better git out of town." Shorty said. "Else we'll be busted, Carl."

"Good idea, but we need some grub."

A stop at the General Store was next. There they bought supplies — a tent, some cooking utensils, some chuck, and an axe. They needed so many things they were bound to forget to buy a few of them. They were starting out farming from scratch.

When finally they drove out of town they had a new team, a new rig, and lots of utensils — and their bank account had taken a severe lacing. They had the plow trailing behind, the discs lifted out of the ground. But the sight to the townspeople was not new — farmers went out each day with rigs like this. They had their saddle-horses tied to the hames of the work-horses, jogging along with dangling stirrups. Suddenly Shorty Madlin smiled.

"What hit you?" Carl asked.

"I was thinkin' of how surprised Gray Blanket and your other broncs will be when they get a collar and harness on them, and not a saddle. My cayuse will sure be plumb worried for a while."

The team jogged along, the saddled horses trotting beside them. They met other rigs coming into town — farmers and their wives and their children. The farmers waved at them and called greetings. They felt as if they belonged already to the community. Tug chains rattled. Steel rims crunched on sand, dust and gravel. Carl felt a laziness creep over him despite the fact there was, in the background, always the ugly memory of Matthew Kalin and the Corporation gunhands.

But when they got a number of miles out of Sulphur Springs there were no farmers. No fences were strung across the prairie with the shiny barbwire glimmering in the hot sun. Some day there would be farmers here, Shorty said; civilization was moving in, and farmers were inching out. The time, he prophesised, was not far away. There would be schools and churches and community halls. Carl listened with half an ear. He was not interested so much in the future five years from now as he was in the immediate future. For if Kalin and the Corporation guns had their way he wouldn't be in this vicinity five years from now. That is, not alive; he might be here, but under six feet.

A big horsefly buzzed in and landed, after some deliberation, on the broad rump of the off-horse. Carl slapped a rein up and down and the horsefly got crushed. He slid off the sleek coat of the horse and hit the dust.

"Ouch!" Carl said.

Shorty looked at him. "The horsefly was

the one to say *ouch,* not you. Or did a thought strike you?"

"Kalin would like to do to me what I did to that horsefly."

"He wouldn't do it, though. Not by himself. He'd send Winn Carter to kill you, or else I'm all wrong."

Carl Hudson shook his head. "You know, I thought Kalin was soft, until I ran into him head-on yesterday at the ranch. That old boy showed me a new light on his dirty character — he's a tough, ruthless man. He tried to knock me down, remember? I never figured he'd ever want to fist fight."

"Maybe you're right, Carl."

"I know I am right."

The sun was sinking lower but the earth radiated heat from its short-grass surface. In the distance, on an alkali bed, a white cone of dust spiralled upward, twisted by the wind. It looked like a miniature tornado which, in reality, it was.

Dusk would stay for a long time after the sun went down. The softness of evening would linger for some hours, as though reluctant to leave the earth. By the time they would reach the O'Reilly farm it would still be dusk.

Both were silent, facing the future and its uncertainties. Carl wondered when the Kalin bunch would hit. He was sure they'd move against the O'Reillys and him and Shorty. It was an ironic feeling. He had been ramrod over these men, and now, so it seemed, he would match his short-gun — or his rifle — against them, to attempt to kill them.

Shorty's voice cut in with, "Fate sure is a funny thing, Carl."

"Whatever drew such a great logic out of your teeming brain, my sawed-off friend?"

"Well, here we are — fightin' the outerfit thet a few days ago paid our wages — and the men we ate with and slept next to are goin' to sling their guns against us, looks like."

"Some of them might," Carl corrected. "And some won't."

"All we kin do," said Shorty, "is wait and see." He dug out the makings and started a cigarette, the seat lurching under him to make the task difficult. "Some of them Bar T boys is right scared of losin' their jobs. They might ride with guns against their old boss an' one of their saddle pals. Mike Hendricks sure is glad that I departed, I'll bet."

"Why?" Carl had a dumb look on his face.

"Why? Ain't you got no brains at all, Hudson? Why, with me gone — he's got the upper hand with Birdie!"

Carl shook his head in sympathy. "Reckon he is glad you left, Shorty."

"Hendricks would ride with Kalin, Mike

would. He'd figger thet way he could get in good with Birdie — helpin' her ol' man, an' playin' the big shot." He fell into a pensive mood. "I should have whup the hell outa Mike Hendricks."

Carl teased him with, "You whip Mike? Mike could beat the livin' daylights out of you with one hand tied behind him and one foot in a washbucket!"

"I knocked him down oncet, rough-housin'. Remember? In the bunkhouse it was, and we got mad and rough."

"He tripped over one of Pancho Wilson's old boots," Carl pointed out.

Shorty looked at him sharply. "You're a-joshin' me," he said. "Wonder if I'll ever see Birdie again, Carl?"

His voice was almost wistful.

Carl found himself glancing at his half-pint partner. For the first time he realized that Shorty Madlin was serious — deadly and earnestly serious. He had been hit and hit hard. Carl at this moment almost felt pity for his partner. Then he realized that Shorty would get over it. But he could hardly blame the short cowpuncher. Birdie had everything — yes, everything — and with this was included a million bucks. But Birdie also had a father — and that father was fat, stupid, and mean. And his name was Matthew Kalin.

And Matthew Kalin did not like Shorty Madlin. Nor did Matthew Kalin cotton to a fellow named Carl Hudson.

"Well," said Shorty, "tonight should be the night, huh?"

"Forty-eight hours will have gone," Carl said.

"No sleep for us tonight, I reckon."

The wagon lurched, sliding into a prairie-dog hole. It lifted and came out on level land again. The dusk was good. Coolness was slowly inching its way across the wilderness. Both were nervous. Small talk did not cover their nervousness. Carl started to joke to break the tension.

"We'll say now you did marry Birdie, Shorty. You two really hooked up in double harness. What would the marriage gain you?"

"A wife — a lovely wife — an' a million bucks."

Carl grinned. "You forget one point."

"An' thet?"

"Kalin would be your father-in-law."

Shorty did not hesitate. "Right off, with that point in mind, I kin see it wouldn't work for a day. Million dollars or no money, it would be no dice. Mebbe in time I might swing around to my right senses again?"

"I sure hope you do."

"You sound kinda disappointed, Carl?"

"Not disappointed, just discouraged about you. The way you're no good to anybody — includin' yourself. When you get normal again I can get work out of you, but not now."

"I cain't be that bad, Carl."

They came off the ridge, horses braced against their breeching straps, and they were down on Wishing Creek. Wind talked in the cottonwood leaves.

"Not far to the O'Reilly camp," Shorty said.

"If it is still there."

"I don't foller you, pard."

"Kalin might have hit them while we were in town."

Shorty stood up and braced his legs wide, steadying himself against the pitch and fall of the wagon as he peered ahead.

"I can see the outerfit," he said. He sat down. "Saw the tip of the barn roof."

When they drove into the O'Reilly farmstead, not a human was in sight. But Carl heard the high whine of the baby crying in the log house. The thought came that this hot weather, while tough on a horse or a human — a grown human — was probably tougher on a little baby. Tired horses were hooked to the plow, over by the barn.

Carl saw the barrel of a rifle sticking out of a hole in a log in the house. He looked at the barn. There a shotgun studied them with a vacant air through a window.

Carl hollered, "Hudson and Shorty Madlin, folks. Your closest neighbors has come to call on you."

The rifle left the hole. John O'Reilly had been behind its trigger. The shotgun pulled back from the window. Janet came out of the barn, the shotgun akimbo under her arm. Carl looked at her and liked what he saw and hoped his emotion kept from showing — which he doubted.

"You sure look good, Miss Janet, but you'd look a might better, Miss, without that thar scattergun."

"We never knew who you two were," the girl explained.

Patsy came out of the house, carrying the baby who had stopped bawling. He was under her arm and he gawked at Carl and Shorty. Carl got an ironic feeling — one sister carried a baby under her arm, the other toted a deadly shotgun. He switched his attention to John O'Reilly.

"What did you say?" the farmer asked.

"What do you mean?" Carl asked, knowing what the farmer was driving at.

"You said somethin' about 'your closest neighbors', meanin' yourself."

Shorty answered that. "We done filed on two homesteads today — down in the Springs.

124

Right south of your south line, O'Reilly."

Patsy said, "Oh, how nice — neighbors," and she looked at her husband, her eyes round and wide. "John, this is wonderful."

Carl looked at Janet. "What do you say?"

"What do you want me to do? Leap up there on that seat and put my arms around you and kiss you? I'm afraid those whiskers might tear my face off."

"I'll gladly shave here and now," Carl said.

But John O'Reilly evidently did not feel like joking. "What is this, a kind of a trick — did you file on the homesteads for yourself, or is your filing for the Kalin spread?"

"Fer us," Shorty said.

Carl said, "Kalin ran us off yesterday," and he told about their run-in with the fat millionaire and Winn Carter. When he told about hitting Kalin in the breadbasket, the farmer almost howled he was so happy. He beat his dusty knee and the dust billowed from his trousers.

Janet looked at Carl. "So you finally got canned, eh?"

"We never got canned. We quit before we got 'discharged', as the millionaires put it. You happy about it?"

"Oh, sure."

Patsy had a wide Irish smile. It seemed to Carl that even the baby gurgled in agreement.

He understood fully what the actions of Shorty and himself had done to bolster the sagging morale of this homesteader family. The minute before, the O'Reillys had been alone — two women and a man and a helpless child — bound by their danger into a close-knit yet fearful group. Now they had two men to side them — good men with rifles, ropes, or short-guns. It was like getting a reprieve from the gallows at the last clocktick. John O'Reilly forgot his tiredness and vigilance. He hollered for Janet to get some beer. This she did, going to the spring on the run.

"You boys camp on this spot," the farmer said. "We gotta stick close together. See you bought a tent in town. Pitch it under them trees over by the barn. Everything we got, men, belongs to you. Here I'll help you unhitch your new team. Darned good pullin'-blood in them hosses, Carl. You sure know how to pick out a horse. Sure good to have you here with us."

"Good to be here," Carl said.

"Lucky to be here," Shorty added.

Carl said, "You go unhook your own horses from that plow, farmer. Your horses have put in a harder day than our broncs. Harder to pull a plow through this dry sod than to pull a wagon acrost the prairie."

"I'll do that. Forgot the tired horses. Gettin'

too dry to plow. Ground won't break over good. We need rain."

"We sure do," Carl said.

"It'll come," Shorty said. He clucked and winked at the baby.

At this moment Janet came with the beer. She and Patsy would unhook the team, she said. Carl asked them to unhook John O'Reilly's team. He was afraid his horses might kick; he did not know them or their tricks as yet.

"You sure got some good help, John," said Shorty.

Carl said, "And dam purty help, too." He tipped his beer bottle, the cold beer soothing his parched throat. "And sure good beer, too."

Shorty sighed, said, "And who wants to go to heaven?"

There was no answer to that, of course.

The women then unhooked the horses from the plow, watered them, and took them into the barn, too, for a mess of hay before turning them loose in the night pasture, an enclosure of about ten acres fenced in so the horses could not wander off in the night.

John O'Reilly, squatting with his back to the cottonwood tree, looked at the baby, who was crawling toward him.

"You men really believe that Kalin will strike?"

Shorty said, "I do."

O'Reilly looked at Carl Hudson. "An' your opinion, Carl?"

"I think he has to hit at us."

O'Reilly shook his head slowly. "I hope not. I'd hate to leave my woman a widder, for one thing. The vigilantes cut loose and turned back that Circle R outfit, like Shorty just told me. You say some of them cowpunchers are in the Sulphur Springs' jail, Shorty?"

"They are. Whole danged outfit under a big peacebond, too. Around fifteen thousand dollars posted. If one of the Circle R hands — or the owner — makes a move against a farmer — even tries to fist-beat him — the outfit forfeits the bond, they tell me. And fifteen thousand is a lot of dough to lose by hittin' a farmer, or anybody else, in the mush."

The women returned. They each got a bottle of beer. Janet sent new bottles around. The beer was hitting Carl, for his belly was empty. It had quite a bit of alcohol, he realized. The women made sandwiches. They drank beer and ate the sandwiches. For the fifth time, Shorty told about Carl burying his fist to the wrist in Kalin's big belly. They all liked that story.

Janet looked at Carl. "What about the girl?" she asked.

"What girl?"

"Birdie Kalin, of course. The one that almost got in a fight with me. If she'd have climbed off that horse I'd have beat her black and blue."

"I don't understand you," Carl said.

Her chin was up. "I thought she was your woman." Carl had to smile at that.

"She sounds like she's a jealous female," Shorty chimed in with a wide smile.

"I am not jealous," Janet said haughtily. "Carl means nothing to me." She caught herself in time and blushed.

Carl said, "Birdie is a dream of the past." He made his words drip loneliness. "A dream that fate has busted. I am innocent."

"All men," declared Patsy, "are always innocent — never guilty. And I speak from years of marriage."

"Yes," her husband said, "years of marriage — about two years, now." From where he stood John O'Reilly could see the brush along the creek and behind them were the rolling hills. "The forty-eight hours are up. Kalin is an uncertain element, one a man cannot bet on. He gave me forty-eight hours to pull stakes. By full sundown, that time is gone."

Carl got to his feet. "No more beer," he told Patsy. "This calls for a clear head and a quick trigger finger. We got to make plans. There'll be a bright moon tonight and that is on our side. But still, it also favors Kalin and the Bar T men. Kalin has to move against us, too."

"Let's make him the boss of this," O'Reilly suggested.

This they did. Carl drew out a plan of campaign. The men would patrol all night. They could catnap in the daytime — if Kalin did not strike on this night. The women went into the root cellar, taking the baby with them. Rifles in hand, the men moved into the brush, and Carl took the slope behind the house. There he sat in the darkness of the high sandstone boulders.

EIGHT

For about an hour there was an inky blackness across the Wyoming rangeland. Somewhere along the creek, evidently perched in a cottonwood tree, was an owl that added solemn and deep hoots to the mystery of the darkness.

The darkness grew thicker and even the owl stopped his hooting. Then the moon came up to bathe the rangelands with golden splendor. The sight thrilled Carl at first, brushing aside the thoughts of danger, but soon this was lost against the push of the predicament and its naked threat of gunsmoke violence. He got to his feet and moved through the rocks, watching the rolling area to the south. From this direction Kalin and Winn Carter and the riders might come, for this was the direction of the big Bar T. Or Kalin might come along Wishing Creek, moving through the brush, his men on foot, bent over rifles, with the buckbrush hiding them.

Hidden in the rocks, Carl looked to the east, following the dark line of trees along the bank of Wishing Creek. But they told him nothing. Shorty was watching this area, for this was his patrol; the little man did not sleep between sougans, as he had wistfully expressed, riding out from Sulphur Springs. He was on the slope above the creek, rifle in his hand and he was hunkered in the shadow of a chokecherry bush, the darkness of the shadow hiding him. Carl looked to the east. Somewhere in the rocks was John O'Reilly. The thought came that the farmer had the most at stake — a wife, a child, a sister — and a chance to build his farm into something substantial. There would be no sougans for O'Reilly, either.

He thought of the women in the root cellar, there in the dark, smelling the strong earth, the dampness of the soil. They would be waiting and listening for the sullen roll of guns against the moonlight, he was sure.

Maybe they had the roughest time of them all.

But he did not know the women had not stayed in the root cellar. Patsy and the baby had gone to look up John O'Reilly and now they were with him on the eastern hill, the baby sleeping back in the rocks, wrapped in blankets. Patsy sat beside her husband, her shotgun in her hand. She watched the dappled, dark-spotted terrain, and wondered if she could have seen a rider — or a rifleman on foot — there in those flickering shadows.

She and her husband said little. When they did they conversed in low tones. They were glad they had two men to side them. With the coming of Shorty and Carl to their side, much of the pressure had been lifted.

"They might not come, husband."

"The forty-eight hours are up."

"That might have been just a bluff. He might have said that to scare you. Remember what happened to the Circle R — the outfit is under peace bond, and some of the men are in jail. The sheriff could do the same to Kalin."

"The Circle R doesn't control millions, like Kalin does. With money a man can do anything, 'cause it pertects him."

"Let's hope he will forget us."

"Kalin will fergit nothin'. You should have seen his face yesterday when I talked to him. Looked like a bloated-up storm-cloud, it did. Wonder he don't sometimes bust a blood vessel when he puffs up like that."

"He might forget us," his wife said, consolingly.

"Where did Janet go?"

"She went to look up Shorty, I think."

But Janet had not gone to visit the sawed-off cowpuncher. She had just told her sister this, and then had gone into the moonlight to look for Carl Hudson. Carl had been back in the rocks, deep in the dark shadows, when she had come up the hill. Carl recognized her immediately. Logic told him no Bar T rider would be so stupid as to blunder openly up the hill. Then his eyes told him that this was a woman, and then he recognized Janet. His heart jumped a little, a thing which surprised him not a bit, and he was glad to see her. But still, there was some of the devil in him, and he decided to have some fun with her.

Accordingly, he waited until she got twenty-feet away. She did not see him for he was securely hidden. She was panting, for the climb was a steep one. Then it was that he spoke in a harsh voice.

"Stop in your tracks, Bar T man. I can recognize you, Mike Hendricks. Put your hands up — forget your holstered gun — or I'll drill you through the brisket."

She stopped in her tracks. Her hands shot up over her head. For a moment, surprise held her, holding back her words. Then her voice came to him in high-pitched terror.

"I'm — Janet — Carl, don't you shoot me!"

Carl grinned. His plan was working. He remained silent for a moment. He wished he could have taken a picture of her standing there in the moonlight with her hands over her head, staring into the darkness at the point where his voice had come from. He deliberately remained silent. And he cocked the hammer on his rifle — this sound was sharp and held danger.

"Don't — don't shoot, you fool. This is Janet."

Carl had had enough fun. "Oh," he said, "I thought you were Mike Hendricks, woman. Come over here and get in the shadows."

She lowered her hands and came close to him. He could not see her face clearly. He decided to have some more fun at her expense.

He didn't know how well — or how bad — this idea would work out.

But he would try it anyway.

He said, roughly, "You fool — why didn't you stay in that root cellar?" and then he grabbed her by her thin shoulders. He turned her and pulled her into his arms and kissed her, hurriedly and damply, on her open mouth.

Then the fireworks started.

The first thing he knew, he was looking at stars. Her open hand had smacked him in the jaw. She could really slap, too. He grinned, chuckled, and let her go. She took another swing at him, her fist closed this time; this hit him on a forearm he had put up for protection. He caught her by both wrists and held her hands.

"Take it easy," he said.

"You — you kissed me!"

He still held her hands. "I know I did. I made a mistake. I thought you was another woman, not Janet O'Reilly."

She stopped struggling. She allowed her wrists to stay in his grip.

Her voice dripped ice. "Who, for instance, did you think I was, Hudson?"

"Birdie Kalin."

"But I am not Birdie Kalin. You kind of let that slip out, didn't you? Down under the trees Birdie was just a 'busted dream', remember?"

"Thought maybe Birdie had rid out to warn us," Carl said. "She used to be kinda in love with Shorty. Figured she might come out ahead of the gunmen, if they come, to warn Shorty, seein' they was oncet so friendly."

"Your stories are sort of crooked, Hudson. She would come out to see Shorty — and you would grab her and kiss her?"

"A little game of ours," Carl said, grinning wickedly. He sure had raised her Irish dander up.

"What do you mean by that, Mister Hudson?"

"When she's around Shorty, he grabs her — when she comes around me, I grab her."

"She must have lived an exciting life."

"Nothin' dull about it," Carl fabricated. "I'll talk it over with Shorty."

136

"You'll talk *what* over with Shorty?"

"Well, you — if you gotta know. We got to have somebody to torment. Now that we ain't got Birdie you'll have to do."

"You mean you'll grab me — both of you — and kiss me?"

"That's the deal."

"I might have something to say about that."

"What you got to say, won't count. Come on over here and sit on this boulder. Easier to argue sitting down, Janet."

They went silently to a flat sandstone rock. He helped her onto it, lifting her, both hands around her thin waist. She remained silent for some moments. He wondered what she was thinking about. She seemed very serious.

He looked at Janet.

"What is on the woman's mind?"

"I'm sorry — I slapped you."

She looked at him. He hugged her around the waist, pulling her momentarily close, then releasing her.

"You're a good woman, Janet."

"Sometimes I'm a bitch — an Irish bitch."

He laughed quietly. "Any woman worth her salt is a bitch sometimes. I don't think there has ever been a wife yet that sometimes didn't hate her husband. I'll bet you'd make a man a nice wife."

"Oh, go on."

"I'll never forget the first time I saw you. A rifle in one hand, a baby under the other arm. You sure looked cute and housewifely like."

"With a rifle? Does a housewife pack a rifle?"

"Most of the time."

"Why?"

"Shoot her husband, I guess."

She sighed. "You're as crazy as a windmill in a cyclone. We're right back where we started. Let's talk serious, huh?"

"About what?"

"Kalin. The Corporation. Will they hit us tonight?"

Carl shrugged. "We've talked that over, Janet. We can only wait. Did you ever hear the story about . . ."

"I don't want to hear a story from you!"

"There's nothing wrong with this. Let me tell you."

"Well, all right."

Carl was glad she had come to sit out the watch with him. They talked in low voices and she chatted avidly after he got her warmed up. He learned a lot about her and, being young, he wondered what was ahead for them — or for him — or for her — as a young man will.

Finally, she slid down off the rock, straightening her dress. "Sis will be worried about me," she said. "Out in the night with wild cowpunchers running loose. I guess I had better go."

"Be daylight in a few hours."

"No, got to go, Carl. Thanks for the nice chat."

"Next time," said Carl, "I'll serve tea. Out of the silver teapot my grandmother on my father's side left me. You bring the tea?"

"And the sugar, too."

"Never did like sugar. I drink my tea without nothin' in it. Want me to go down the hill with you?"

"Your job is to stay here and watch. You can't see anything from the bottom of the hill. Good night."

"Well," said Carl, "we spent our first night together."

"Oh shut up."

He watched her go down the slope. The memory of Birdie Kalin, which once had been rather strong, now faded into limbo, and her million bucks went with it. Homesteading next to the O'Reillys might prove interesting, at that. He watched her until she was out of sight in the moonlight, which was when she entered the shadows of the cottonwoods, almost in the farmstead yard. He did this for two reasons. First, he wanted to keep his eyes on her; second, he wanted to determine just how far a distance he could detect a human figure in the moonlight. He went back to nursing his thoughts and trying to keep awake.

False dawn came in, and he was very sleepy; one thing, though, helped him — with the false dawn came a high chill down from the western peaks, miles away, but still covered with snow. This cut through him and kept sleep away.

The dawn strengthened, then darkened, and within a few minutes the sun showed over the hills. It was red and ugly and told of a day of hard heat. There was not a cloud in the sky. The range was barren of riders and on a hill, about two miles south, he saw two cattle — his rangeman's eyes told him they were cattle, not horses. They were grazing along the crest of the hill for here there was still some grass, though dried and short it was. When the sun progressed higher and heat got more rigid they would wander with their calves down to the creek bottom and spend the hot and long afternoon bedded-down under the cottonwoods, enjoying the shade. Carl gave the range a long and slow and deep look, using his field glasses — but he saw no riders. Kalin would not hit, he figured, in the daylight; still, there would have to be a guard. Vigilance was the word. He went down the hill, rubbing his whiskers: When had he shaved last, he wondered idly. Shorty came through the brush, rifle in hand; weariness oozed from the sawed-off.

"We went past the deadline," he said.

Carl nodded.

"Don't seem like Kalin."

"Sure doesn't."

"You ain't very talkative, Carl."

"Sleepy."

"I had a visitor toward mornin'."

"Mister Matthew Kalin?" Carl joked.

"Janet."

"Try the hug and grab and kiss on her?"

"I did."

"What did she do?"

"Busted me on the kisser. Almost knocked me down. She can hit like a mule kin kick."

Carl rubbed his jaw. It still ached a little.

"She said you had pulled it on her afore I did," Shorty lamented. "She was all ready for me and she laid the timber on me."

"Good," Carl said.

Shorty looked at him. His big eyes were bloodshot from lack of sleep. His whiskers, despite his youth, had a touch of gray. He looked like a bum who had just been booted out of a boxcar.

"You talk to your old, old sidekick that way," he lamented.

141

Carl said nothing, merely smiling. He was glad the night was over. Heat was forming, building in layers, and the cold chill was gone, broken and smashed by the sun. They came to the farmstead. Janet was boiling coffee, the smell strong and good; Patsy was frying hot cakes, and the baby slept in his crib. John O'Reilly came out of the brush.

"We should stake out a guard," the farmer said. "They might be watching us from some hill and seein' we have nobody out . . ."

Janet said, "You men are dead tired. I had a little sleep. I'll go up on the hill where Carl was, and after you all eat get some sleep."

Carl looked at her, thanking her with his eyes.

"Take my rifle," Carl told her.

She got the rifle from its position by the tree and went into the heat. Carl looked at his companions. They were a sleepy, tired-looking bunch. Men with whiskers and blood-shot eyes; Patsy weary from a night of little rest. He found himself wishing that Janet would not wander around at night. He decided to lecture both of the women and make them stay in the root cellar this coming night. He knew that Kalin would strike, but he did not know *when*. Kalin was playing a rough tough game and he was loading it with suspense that ate into them and left them raw and nervous.

They ate breakfast, and it was a good breakfast, too. Bacon, home cured, fried just right; gallons of hot coffee; stacks of brown wheat cakes and homemade syrup. Shorty Madlin said, "Remember the rotten chuck at the Bar T, Carl?"

"I might forget it," Carl said, "but my belly can't."

"If home life is anythin' like this," Shorty told the world, "I aim to get hooked up double right pronto."

"Got to find a woman first," Carl said, "and I doubt if any woman — even an ol' maid — would want you."

"My friend," Shorty said. "My boosom friend."

NINE

After eating, Carl stretched out in the shade, lying on an old quilt. Within a few minutes, despite his wishes, he was sleeping. Shorty Madlin beat him to it, though, for Shorty was snoring softly before sleep took Carl. When Carl awakened, the afternoon heat was on — it hung to the earth and bent the trees with its invisible weight. He was wet with sweat, his clothes hanging to his sparse frame. He sat up and looked at Shorty, who was still asleep.

He felt a little ashamed of himself. He looked around and saw nobody. A glance at his Ingersoll watch showed it was three o'clock. The thought came that perhaps all this time Janet was still on guard. This was not fair, for she was tired and sleepy, too.

Roughly he shook his partner awake. "Get out of the dark, you ugly stiff. Think you'll sleep your life away."

Shorty sat upright hurriedly. "They — they comin'?"

"No, they ain't comin' — not thet we know of, right off. But you been sleepin' while the rest of us has been working."

Sleep ran out of Shorty's eyes. He stretched and yawned. "Gawd, another scorchin' hot day. You jes' come awake yourself. I feel refreshed. Now, if I had some vittles . . ."

"Always thinking of your belly."

Carl straightened. He went into the cabin, leaving Shorty behind him, sitting on the old quilt. Patsy was sleeping in the corner on the bed, her baby beside her. The baby was awake. The baby looked at Carl with wide, baby eyes. Carl went outside. Was Janet still on the rimrock? He climbed the hill. The heat bore down, thick and oppressive across the hills, the heaving heat waves could be seen, sucking what little moisture there was out of the earth. Carl realized that dry land farming would be a hard venture here. The farmer would be at the mercy of the Rain God. Irrigation from deep wells or from dams in creeks was the answer. He was sure of that. Wishing Creek never went dry. He and Shorty had a lot of hard work ahead of them. Work with a fresno moving dirt to build their dam and their dikes and canals. Work to build ditches to get water out onto alfalfa fields and grain fields. Already he yearned for the backbreaking good toil. He went through the rocks, the boulders rearing on each side; here it was a little cool. He found Janet sleeping on her side, her head on her right arm, her hair spilled out. Beside her was her rifle. He grinned and squatted beside her.

She slept in peace, her heavy breast rising and falling under her blue shirt. She had a patch on the shirt on the back. Her eyes were closed, the lids blue-veined, and her mouth was open slightly.

Silently he lifted the rifle and moved it to one side. Then he got his handkerchief from his pocket and held the tip of it just so it brushed her nose. She batted at it, thinking it was a fly; he grinned in boyish devilment. She kept on sleeping. Again the handkerchief tip tickled her nose; again she batted — this time, though, he was not quick enough and she grabbed the handkerchief, coming instantly awake.

She sat up and looked at him.

"You, huh?"

"Me," Carl said, "and my little handkerchief."

"I thought you were a fly."

"I am not made to fly. I have no wings."

She got to her feet. "And from what I'd judge off-hand, you never will get wings — for where you'll go they issue pitchforks, not wings. Good Lord, I must have been asleep."

"Some guard." Carl chided.

"My brother is back in the rocks," she said. "He slept a while and then left you two bums sleeping — so he told me — so it made not one bit of difference whether I slept or not."

"No justice," Carl said, sadly wagging his head.

She stretched and her shirt gaped open a little, revealing something. Carl liked what he saw. She noticed this and she stuck out her tongue in girlish disdain.

"Just like all men."

Carl said, "We'd better get to work."

She looked at him. "Work? At what?"

Carl rubbed his whiskers. It sounded like a farmer filing a mower sickle. "They might hit tonight. We got to be ready for them."

They found John O'Reilly back in the rocks. He had slept for a few hours, he said, and he had not had enough rest. He was nervous and dirty and unshaven, but it was his raw nerves that showed the most. He was worried and worried sick, Carl saw.

They squatted in the shade and talked. Carl told Janet that she and her sister and baby would have to stay in the root cellar. No wandering around like last night, he warned.

"We don't want to be helpless, if the fight starts. In other words, we want to help, Carl."

Carl nodded. "Only logical, woman. But that root cellar is not level with the ground. Two bottomwood logs are between the roof and the earth. Cut a section out of a log on each side and poke your weapons through the hole."

"Good idea," she said, brightening.

Carl said, "Though I sure don't cotton to the idea of havin' women partake in a gun fight."

"Pioneer women have fought side by side with their men for years," she said angrily.

"I know that, but I ain't your man," he corrected. "So you keep in thet root cellar and fight from there if needs be."

"I'll get a saw and saw out the log to make a lookout hole," she said.

"Take the crib in there with you," John O'Reilly ordered, "and keep the baby there, savvy?"

"Hope he doesn't catch a cold."

"Hope he doesn't stop a bullet," the father said. "He might get over a cold, but not a bullet."

"Oh what a terrible thought," she said and went down the slope.

Carl and the farmer squatted in the shade and made plans for the attack that might come — or might not come. They decided to fight the Bar T men on the farmstead proper, inside the yard. Make them come out of the brush to them. The buildings were far enough from the timber to make it impossible for a man to hide in the brush and toss a burning-brand onto a building, setting it on fire. All of the buildings had sod roofs, and soil would not burn, of course. This was one good point in their defense. They thought of drilling holes in the log barn and putting lengths of pipe in the holes, for the farmer said he had some half-inch pipe. They could cut this into lengths, insert these in the holes, and they would look like rifle barrels. But they would fight from the house.

Carl said, "Good idea. You go down and dig the holes with your brace and bit. I'll get Shorty up here on guard. I got some riding to do."

"Riding? Where?"

"I'm going to scout ahead and watch the Bar T from Thunder Mountain. That is a few miles this side of the ranch. I got my field glasses and if they come, I'll ride in ahead of them."

"Good idea."

Carl returned to the farmstead where he saddled his horse and rode out, but he was only a mile or so from the O'Reilly ranch when he heard a horse coming fast from behind him. He turned on his stirrups and his scowl of puzzlement changed to one of happiness which he soon hid under a look of anger.

"Where do you figure you're going, woman?"

"With you, of course," Janet O'Reilly said. Her temper flared at his tone of voice. "Don't think you can order me around, Carl Hudson!"

"I can get off this bronc, put you acrost my knee, and paddle your purty behind, and don't forget that! I don't need any company — let alone a sleepy female who goes to sleep on guard."

"You forget I slept because my brother was back in the rocks watching instead of me," she said.

Carl said, "You win, girl."

They jogged over the hills, for the sun was too hot for speed — their mounts, even at this slow pace, were rimmed with sweat.

Then they saw in the distance a buggy heading out of the Bar T, a team of splendid sorrels hooked to its double-trees, the roustabout handling the ribbons, and somebody on the seat beside him. Carl focused his glasses on the buggy and lowered them with, "Birdie Kalin an' Sam, the roustabout. Prob'ly headin' for Willow Bend."

But the buggy, when it came to the fork, did not take the Willow Bend road, which went southeast; instead, it turned on the lesser-used road, the Sulphur Springs road.

"Goin' to the railhead," Carl had mused. "Wonder what Birdie aims to do in Sulphur Springs?"

"If you are so worried about Miss Kalin, why don't you ride down and talk to the beautiful millionairess?"

"I do believe you are jealous."

"Me? Jealous? Humph!"

"I'm going to do just that."

"But I won't go with you!"

"Dare you to."

"Oh, none of that boy stuff."

"Anybody who wouldn't take a dare would suck eggs."

"Oh, all right — I'll go along, but if we get in a fight . . ."

"Ladies don't fight, remember?"

"I am no lady — at some times."

When she saw them coming, Birdie Kalin had old Sam pull in the team, and they waited until Carl and Janet rode close. When she saw Carl, Birdie smiled. That smile changed to a light scowl when she recognised Janet O'Reilly.

"Card Hudson," she said lightly. "Since when did you and Miss O'Reilly become such good friends? Out here in the wilderness — just the two of you — and you never would take me riding alone. Why, I'm beginning to suspect . . ."

"Whatever you suspect," Janet said, "just keep to yourself, Miss Kalin."

Birdie looked at her. Janet looked at Birdie.

Sparks began to fly and simmer. Carl cut in quickly with, "Where you heading, Birdie?"

"For Sulphur Springs, of course."

"Leaving?" Carl looked significantly at the dozen or so suitcases piled neatly in the rear of the buggy.

"Going back to New York. I'll miss you," Carl said, and he meant it.

"I'll miss you, too. And Shorty. How he ran after me. Where is the little runt?"

"Back in the hills."

"What's he doing back there?" She frowned prettily, still keeping a wary eye on Miss O'Reilly.

"We took up homesteads."

"You did! Then that means you're really an enemy of the Old Man's. He still hasn't forgiven you for hitting him in that pot belly of his. He and I had a fight. So, back to New York I go."

"Does your father intend to run off us O'Reillys?" Janet asked.

"Wouldn't you like to know?" Birdie spoke with syrupy smoothness. She smiled at Carl. "When you get to New York look me up, you big sap. Okay, old man, hit those hay burners and let's get down the road."

The buggy moved on, and the girl did not look back. Carl shoved back his hat, wiped sweat from his forehead with the palm of his hand, and grinned. Janet's voice cut into his amusement.

"What are you smiling about, you big ape?"

"She sure laid you out with one blow."

"Nothing but a hussy. A rich hussy."

"And she told us nothing," Carl said. "Nothing we already didn't know." He looked at the buggy already almost lost against the wilderness expanse. "When she marries the gent she hooks up with he is going to know he has to stand punishment for those millions of dollars he might think he will get for simply hooking up with her. I'd hate to be in his shoes."

"Thought you liked her?"

"I do — to a certain degree." Carl looked at the girl. "Say, we're going to live a hard married life, Janet — already you pick on me."

"I wouldn't marry you if you were the last man on earth."

"That is what my mother once told my father, if I remember what the old man said rightly. We'd best mosey along."

"That is the smartest thing you have said yet!"

They came finally to Thunder Mountain. Actually, it was not a mountain — it was a butte. It reared its blackness out of the foothills and was about six hundred feet in altitude, its sides steep in some areas and slanting in others. Igneous rocks, black and big, rested on its sides; there was a sort of a trail up the north side, Carl knew, for he had ridden this country many, many times. They tied their horses on the east slope in a thicket of serviceberry bushes. There the sun did not hit the broncs and they were hidden. Then, carrying a rifle and field glasses, they ascended the slope, Carl in the lead.

The trail was rough in some spots, and Carl helped Janet over a few barriers; both were breathing hard when, at long last, they reached the summit. The top of the butte was about a quarter mile long east and west and about a hundred yards wide north and south. The Bar T ranch was to the south. So they crossed the flat area, the wind blowing against them, and they gained the high rocks on the south slope, and here they stopped and Carl said, "This is the spot."

"Oh," the girl said, "how beautiful."

Because of their high altitude the rangelands tumbled away on all sides, and in the west you could see the dim outlines of the mountains, looking more like clouds than material elements. The hills ran away, tumbling in all directions; cattle and horses were mere specks on the sun-browned hills. Carl liked the happy look on the girl's face.

He watched her as she watched the terrain

below, the wonder of its great expanse showing on her suntanned, girlish face. Her eyes finally came to rest on the buildings comprising the Bar T.

"Is that — the Kalin ranch?"

"Sure is," Carl said. "That is where the big shaggy fat wolf lives in his den."

Carl glanced at the sun and guessed it was around three o'clock. Janet focused the field glasses, training them on the ranch below them.

"Doesn't seem to be much stirring," she said. "The heat must be holding everybody inside the house and the bunkhouse, because there seems to be only one man — he's at a small building, doing something to a horse's hoof, looks like."

Carl nodded. "The blacksmith shop, maybe. Shoeing a horse." He got the glass, turning the adjusting-screw, and the ranch came into clear relief, complete with buildings and haystack and barns.

About an hour later, a rider appeared below the butte, on the west side. He was heading south for the big ranch. He had come from the direction of Wishing Creek.

Carl whistled softly.

"Who is that?" she asked.

The glasses identified the man. "Mike Hendricks," Carl said. "Well, I'll be . . . He must have ridden over to spy on our outfit. Now he is coming back with his report."

"But we never saw him."

"Big country," Carl said. "Lotsa square miles of range. Wonder if he seen us? Hope he didn't."

"I wonder if he knows we are on this butte?"

Carl shook his head. "I doubt it, Janet. Anyway, he's headin' into the ranch, and now he's goin' into the office."

A man came out of the barn and took Hendricks' horse to the watering-trough, then to the barn. Both man and horse disappeared into the dark confines of the building which Carl knew so well. Hendricks was inside the office for quite a while. Carl judged the time to be about ten minutes. He kept his glasses on the front door of the building. When Hendricks came out, two men came out with him, and they stood on the shady long porch, talking. Carl could not see them clearly because the porch cast a shadow. But he knew, from their outlines, that one was the gunman, Winn Carter. And the other — the bulky one — was none other than his Money Bags, the millionaire Matthew Kalin.

Hendricks went to the bunkhouse.

Winn Carter and Money Bags went back into the house. Then the ranch was quiet again. Men trooped to the mess shack. He counted only four hands. Then he got the significance of the deal.

"The others don't want to ride against women and a baby," he said. "They must have been fired and pulled stakes."

"Hope you are right, Carl."

"Sure looks that way to me."

They waited and hunger arose in them. But there was nothing to eat, unless they dined off the sparse dried grass — and their stomachs, and appetites, were not meant for bovine fare. After eating, the men came out of the bunkhouse and went to the barn. They led out horses and saddled them in the compound. Carl watched and saw that they saddled two extra horses. His heart beating, he looked at Janet, who now had the glasses.

"They aim to ride," he said.

She handed him the glasses.

Her voice was a little high-pitched. "You look, Carl. And talk to me, telling me what you see."

"All right."

She watched his face. The distance was too far for naked eyesight; also, the dusk was beginning to come in. The sun had gone down, and still the heat held the earth — radiating upward from the parched, burned soil.

"Two men are comin' from the house. They carry rifles, I see. I suppose they have short-guns, too — but I can't see, of course."

"Yes."

"They're going to the four men who saddled horses. The others are in leather now, waiting."

"Who are they?"

"I can't see for sure. Distance and the sun has set . . . But they could only be two men."

"Winn Carter," she breathed.

"Yes, and Matthew Kalin. They're getting into their saddles, and a cowpuncher is holding Kalin's horse — takes him some time to get his lard between the fork and the cantle. He must really want revenge. He's gonna ride twenty-odd miles, something I've never seen him do before."

"They're heading out of the ranch, aren't they?"

"Yes."

"Which way?"

"Well, the road runs east a mile or so, then they come to the fork. One road runs south to Willow Bend; the other, north toward Sulphur Springs. We got to wait and see."

"Oh, I hope they don't turn north!"

Carl had no answer to that. He figured he knew full well which way the Kalin gunmen would turn when they came to the fork — and it would not be south. Kalin and Carter, so it looked like, headed the six men — they thundered out of the yard, and for a moment the cottonwood trees along the road hid them. They appeared spasmodically as they rode through the trees, hidden one moment, visible dimly the next. They rode fast, too.

"They're at the fork, Janet."

"Which way — are they turning, Carl?"

He did not answer for some time. He watched the six come to the fork, and then, of one accord, their broncs headed north, headed on the trail that led to Sulphur Springs — and the Wishing Hills.

He lowered his glasses.

His voice was husky. "They're headin' north. They aim to hit at us — tonight, girl."

"Oh, my God!"

TEN

For a moment, they looked at each other, and during that moment neither spoke. A cricket chirped back in the rocks. That was the only sound — and beyond this sound was the whispering silence of the gigantic wastelands. There was a moment of dreadful apprehension and then Carl was on his feet.

"We got to ride like hell to get ahead of them, girl. We got a few miles of lead on them. Us for our saddles."

"Our horses are tired. Their broncs are fresh."

Carl said, on the run, "They won't ride too fast. They want to hit in moonlight. Besides, from this butte to our camp is about fifteen miles or so, and they have to cover about twenty."

"Hurry, Carl."

They came to the dim trail that led downward to their saddle-horses. The trail now was in darkness, being on the east side, but Carl hurried down it, the girl behind him. Once she fell and he heard the rattle of shale, the sound of her boots on loose gravel; he turned and caught her, steadying her. Her hands were in his, her body against his. And he felt the softness of her. It was a moment of calm, and the significance of it touched them both.

"Be careful, Janet."

"All right, Carl."

He took it slower. Logic told him that the Bar T men would want fresh horses when they made their escape from the O'Reilly ranch. Behind them, they expected to leave smoke, flame and death — they wanted fast horses to make good their escape. That meant, then, they would not ride too fast, on their way to the scene of their crime.

Yes, and they needed another ally, an ally not yet in the sky. The round, yellow Wyoming moon.

Now the steepest part of the trail was behind. Carl had cut his palm on rock, and he was glad it was his left palm, not his right — he handled his six-shooter with his right hand, and, if this went to close quarters, a six-shooter might decide this issue — decide it for once and for all. He was glad when the bottom of the butte reared up and he walked on level land. He turned and asked, "How did you make it, Janet?" and she said, breathlessly, "I skinned my knee."

"Which one?" he asked, still teasing.

"The right one."

"Want me to stop and look at it?"

"Oh, don't josh me now. This is serious."

"Here are our horses," he said and grinned.

She mounted quickly, and he swung into leather, his horse rearing against the savage constraint of the bit. She was already riding north, her mount running freely. She was new to this country but evidently she was not new to a saddle, for she rode like an old-timer — bent forward on the stirrups, her horse running with reins at the right tension.

Carl had to use his spurs to catch her. She was riding too fast, and he did not want her to run the wind out of her horse: so he put his mount even with hers, and he shouted to be heard above the sound of their horses' hoofs.

"Take it easy, woman. We got about fifteen miles ahead of these horses, and we don't want them to go down on us."

She pulled in and looked at him. They got to a trail lope, that mile-eating pace of the range-pony — easy to ride and quick to cover the miles.

She said, "There is a short cut, isn't there?"

"Yes."

"Where is it?"

He said, "We won't ride it."

Sweat was on the broncs. Sweat rimmed the edges of their saddle blankets, was under the headstalls, hung in green-ropes from the shanks of their bits. She looked at him.

"Why not?"

"Too dangerous."

She kept her eyes on him. "How many miles will it cut off, Carl?"

He gave the brief thought. Then, "Oh, about five, maybe almost six."

"We ride it," she said. "I know where it is. Walker Canyon cutoff, they call it. I've seen the trail from the other end — it runs along the canyon high in the air. I'm not afraid."

Carl shook his head.

"We need to save every minute," she hollered, bent low. "We got to warn them, get ready — Carl, we have to take it."

She was right and he knew it. Still, he was not afraid for himself, for he had ridden the canyon trail before, although in the daylight; he was worried about her safety.

One misstep by a horse, one trip over a rock, and over the edge a horse would go, sliding, squealing, screaming, to his death — and the death of his rider — down into dark Walker Canyon.

"We got to take it, Carl."

He swung his mount to the west a little and said, "All right, girl. But ride easy — and ride light in your stirrups — and be ready to kick free of your mount the minute he even acts like he is going to stumble."

"I'll do that, Carl."

The thought came to him — warm and good — that she had what it took to make a pioneer wife. She had, above everything else, courage — and that was what this raw country needed — raw courage. He knew there would be a gunfight ahead. And, being practical, he did not think beyond that time, for bullets, he knew, had a way of killing a man, regardless of his age, wealth, education, or station in life.

He figured it was about two miles to Walker Canyon. The idea now was to get there before it grew too dark, for with darkness on the high trail, the danger would be intensified. The trail, he figured, was about half a mile long, a perpendicular trail almost, leading down on Wishing Creek — coming out on the source of the creek, there in the painted badlands.

"Drive your horse hard," he hollered.

She was riding Shorty Madlin's horse, and for this he was thankful — the horse was fast, young, and sure-footed. From the corner of his eye he watched her quirt rise and fall. They swept across the prairie, hoofs making an insistent drumming sound against the dried and lonesome earth. Carl held his horse back a little. Neither spoke again until they came to the trail down into Walker Canyon.

And then both drew rein, looking down the narrow treacherous trail.

Their horses breathed heavily, stirrup leathers rising and falling, and saddle leather creaked occasionally. Carl gave the trail a quick, hard glance. He wanted to make sure no boulders had tumbled down to block the narrow path that twisted downward, hanging on the edge of the canyon. But darkness held most of the trail, for the lip of the canyon cut off what little twilight there was, and his glance told him nothing.

He looked at her.

She looked at him.

Her eyes were steady and her lips moved slowly when they said, "All right with me, Carl. Lead the way."

"One thing first," he said.

"And that?"

He shook down his forty foot catchrope, getting the kinks out of it. He handed her the lasso end.

"Put this round your saddle-horn, Janet. I'll tie the other end hard-and-fast to my saddle-horn. Then, if one of us slips — loses his horse — the other might hold him. But if I slip, leave your saddle fast, let the horse shift for himself, for he might be dragged over the ridge."

"Good idea."

He himself tied the rope to the horn of her saddle, pulling the twine secure and hard.

"Ride about twenty feet behind me. Here, take the rope, and keep it coiled, playing it out if I get too far ahead, but don't let me hit the end of it — to do that might jar both our broncs off the trail."

"You watch how far you ride ahead," she warned.

He squeezed her hand. "All right, let's go, child."

His horse did not want to take the treacherous trail. He dodged, turned, reared, but Carl used his quirt and spurs, driving rebellion out of the beast. Then the animal, seeing he could not evade the issue, took to the trail and the treacherous down-hill trip began.

Carl hollered back occasionally, sometimes not daring to look back at her, but he always got a cheery reply — although sometimes that reply was given in a shaky tone of voice. He warned her not to look over the edge — the abyss was black and seemingly endless. This she said she would not do; instead, she would look at the canyon wall on her right. Carl occasionally glanced over the ridge, but even his heart pounded harder. The thought came that they should not have taken the perilous path. But they could not turn back; they were on it; a horse could not turn on this narrow aisleway down the side of the mountain. Then, his heart froze.

Behind him, he heard a scuffle — hoofs pounded on rock and then the rock slid. He was halfway out of saddle, going out on the wrong side — the right side — and then, on glancing back, he saw her bronc had not slid — he stood behind the rump of his own horse.

"That was a boulder — sliding down behind us — scared my horse and he jumped . . ."

"We're halfway down it," he said.

"Let's go on."

"You're a brave girl."

"Oh, I'm not brave — I just lack brains, and when a person is dumb, he doesn't realize the danger."

Carl grinned, despite the gravity of the situation. "Reckon that's right," he said, righting himself in the saddle, his heart back to normal. "All right — ahead we go — watch the slack in the rope."

They made their horses walk. To trot a horse might prove disastrous. The half-mile seemed, to Carl, to be about ten miles. They inched down the trail, her horse ten feet behind his; the darkness thickened as they descended deeper into the canyon. Carl tried not to let unrest tear him. This short-cut would save them some miles. Despite their slow pace because of the danger, they were still saving time. But would this canyon trail ever come to its weary end?

"All right, Janet?"

"Okay, Carl."

"Not far now. Maybe a furlong."

"How long," she asked, "is a furlong?"

"One-eighth of a mile. I can see the flat land at the mouth of the canyon. There is more light ahead of us."

"We did right by going this way."

"Not over yet."

"Don't be so pessimistic. But I sure am glad I am riding Shorty's horse. One of our old horses — they are all work-horses — might get tangled up in his big hoofs, and blotto."

"Blotto," Carl said.

Horse, brace yourself, dig in your shod front hoofs, balance yourself with your steel-shod hind hoofs. Watch yourself in that shale, for shale had slid across the trail. Steady, boy, steady. Good boy, now to look back, to see if Janet's horse can go across the slide-area.

Steady, horse, steady. Yes, put down your head, smell the shale, study it in the darkness. That's the way, boy — take your time, lift your hoofs high, and walk across it. Steady in the saddle, woman.

You're across it, horse. Good horse!

Carl put his attention again on the road

ahead. A glance to his left told him they were nearing the end, for he could see the bottom of the canyon — something impossible to see when halfway down. They rounded a bend, a rock fell off the lip; it did not fall far, though, like the rock had done back higher on the rimrock trail. And then, suddenly, they were on the rolling bottomlands, the trail behind them, the canyon yawning at their backs.

"We made it, Carl!"

There was high color in her face. It glistened in her eyes, added excitement to her voice, and gave him a new insight into her character. To this woman, life had zest; to her, life would never grow dull. But this was not the time, or the place, for such thoughts.

"Loosen the catch-rope?"

She untied the rope and he coiled it, all the time loping toward Wishing Creek camp. Now it was downhill all the way, just follow the creek. He strapped his rope to the right side of the saddle's fork and said, "Now to ride, woman."

"With you, Carl."

They streaked down the trail, dust behind them. She put her horse close to his, and her words were clear, "We made it easy, didn't we?"

"Sure did."

"I'm afraid, Carl."

Carl looked at her. The dusk did not hide her eyes — they were not bright now, for she was thinking of six riders — men who rode with their short-guns naked in their fists, with rifles riding high in saddle boots, stocks up.

"So am I," he confessed.

They had about four or five miles to go to reach the O'Reilly farmstead. They went over the land on which Carl and Shorty had yesterday filed homestead entries, and the bitter thought came to Carl that he might never put a plow to this land, might never boost a log into place on the house he planned to build. He tried to shove those thoughts into the discard, but they would not go.

When they came into the yard, Shorty came running down off the rocks. They scattered dust and gravel, and John O'Reilly, who had run out of the barn, rifle in hand, jumped back to escape from being peppered.

"What is it, Carl?"

"They're coming. Six of them."

Patsy said, "Oh my God," and her face was pale, her voice trembling. She looked at her husband, at her baby in her arms, and then at her sister. "How far behind are they?"

Janet said, "How far, Carl?"

"They might have covered half the distance.

But I figure they won't hit until the moon is up, anyway. You got to see to shoot a shortgun or rifle, you know. Shorty, Kalin rides with them."

"You don't say."

"Winn Carter, too. And your old friend, Mike Hendricks. I saw Birdie. She was getting the roustabout to take her to Sulphur Springs and the railroad. She said to say hello."

"Oh."

Carl was dismounting, and Janet came off her saddle, too.

"We'd better get ready," Carl said crisply.

ELEVEN

They came when the moon rode high in the cloudless Wyoming sky.

First, they sent in a man on foot. He left his bronc in the brush and he disappeared for a moment, hidden by the rocks, and then he reappeared again, among other rocks.

Janet said, "A scout, Carl."

They were on the hill. The man was about three hundred yards away — a blot of darkness in moonlight.

"Lookin' the place over," Carl said. "The others are back in the brush. Now you get for that root cellar, and get there fast."

"I want to watch."

"You go. I want to pepper him with my rifle. And he might shoot back. Make tracks, woman."

"You — be careful, Carl."

"I sure will, Janet."

She looked at him. Moonlight washed across her, showing her face plainly, adding to the captivating lure of her full, well-built body. Then she turned and went out of sight, the rocks hiding her.

Carl brought his rifle to his shoulder. He

tried to find his sights, but it was difficult; he had little chance of hitting the man who had pulled back in the rocks. Carl shot three times, the lever working, the rifle kicking back.

A bullet lanced back at him, coming to the right of where he had fired; he switched his target, and fired again — but then another shot came, winging overhead, and this came from the buckbrush, back of the boulders. This told him the Bar T man was running back to Kalin and Winn Carter.

Carl grinned and reloaded his Winchester. He had not heard the whine of the man's bullets. Of course, his own Winchester had been talking, but he figured the man had missed by many feet, and he knew he had done likewise.

He knew the other five Bar T riders — including Matthew Kalin and Winn Carter — were down Wishing Creek, for he had glimpsed them riding in under the moonlight. He wondered what plan of attack Kalin would use. He knew what the man's methods would be — they would be ruthless. He was ruthless. Only this time he was not ruthless with dollars, he was ruthless with fellow humans. He would hit and hit hard and fast, wanting to get this over with, and to get out of this section. He would kill everybody he could — even the baby — he had to kill them all. Then nobody would be left to lay the finger of testimony in his direction. The sheriff could prove nothing. But word would go out to other homesteaders — stay off the Kalin Corporation Bar T outfit — or you die, sodbuster.

The muscles along Carl's throat jumped with monotonous regularity. It always did that in times of stress and tension. His thoughts went to Janet. By now she should be in the root cellar. Patsy and the baby were in the root cellar, too. They had a shotgun. They would crouch there in the dark, the damp smell of the raw earth in their nostrils, the feel of the logs rough on their hands. They would watch through the sawed-out section in the logs, and they would hear the sullen roll of the rifles, the throaty roar of the .45s. And fear — naked, terrible fear — would be clutching them, tearing at them. The fear of death for a loved one.

But he knew he could not keep his mind on death. He hoped he would come out alive. For a moment, the thought of death was in him; it drove its shaft deep, and he felt fear — rough and ugly fear. This passed, for he made it pass, and he put his mind on the task ahead.

There was a hard wind from the east. It whipped across the hills, bending the cottonwood tress and the box elders and willows, and it dimpled the buckbrush, sending it bending in rippling waves of resiliency. It was an ally for Kalin and his gun-raiders. It hid the sound they would make. It created other sounds — like those in the rocks — and these sounds could be mistaken for the advance of a man, the sound of him and his coming.

He felt anger toward the Sulphur Springs sheriff. But then he realized a man could not be arrested on suspicion; to incur arrest, he had to be guilty of some direct violation of the law, not some suspected violation. But this was of small importance, also. The main thing was that Kalin and his men were out to burn this spread to the ground, to kill its owners, to kill two former Bar T men, even its old ramrod.

After Janet and Carl had come into the farmstead, the five of them had held a council of war, and Carl had been appointed a sort of "general". He had changed his plans, he told them — instead of staying in the buildings and fighting for them, the three men — Shorty, John and he — would take to the brush, fighting the way an Indian fights, slinking, watching, peering, shooting, moving. The women would hide in the root cellar for it was imperative they stay out of the way of bullets, if possible.

"If you men go down," Janet had said, "Patsy and I will fight until we get killed."

John O'Reilly had shifted his pipe in his mouth, looking at his baby. "No need to talk that way," he consoled. "We're out to win, sister."

"We got to win," Patsy declared, with more emphasis than certainty.

Carl was on the hill, just south of the house, John O'Reilly was on the west hill, just back of the root cellar. Shorty Madlin was on the south hill, back of the barn. They had even concocted a password to be hollered so they could be sure not to shoot at one of their own fellows. This password was a single word: *Sodbusters*.

Suddenly Carl stiffened, looking toward the east. There, in that direction, had suddenly come flame — a lifting, red stab against the moonlight. He knew right away what had happened.

The Bar T raiders had lit fire to the underbrush.

Instantly the entire area was ablaze. Gaunt cottonwoods, flame licking up their trunks, were outlined against the sky, their green leaves becoming seared by the darting, flickering tongues of scarlet. The wind whipped in, and the flame ran through the dried brush, sending out huge clouds of black smoke.

Carl saw through the manoeuver immediately. The smoke would whip across the farmstead, building a dim screen of darkness, and, under this, they would advance. They would come in, crouched over their guns, the smoke screening them. This put a new light on this fight, Carl realized. With this realization came the grim concrete fact that Kalin was out to win — to kill — under any circumstances.

A moment of thought told him the fire would not reach the farmstead proper. John O'Reilly had prudently cleared an area between the creek and his buildings, evidently preparing for just such an incident at the time of preparation being, of course, in case of accidental fire, not deliberate human action — outright arson. So the farmer had plowed a strip of land between his buildings and the underbrush; this area was clear of inflammable brush and trees, and was about a hundred feet wide. This would keep the fire from jumping to the buildings, but it would not keep the smoke from rolling in and hiding the buildings.

Carl knew there was only one thing to do: that was to go down into the smoke, and fight in the compound around the buildings, for Kalin and his men would go in under the cover of the smoke and set fire to the buildings. He figured that Shorty and John O'Reilly would also go down, for it was plain to all what Kalin's plan of action was.

Another thing, also in favour of Kalin, was apparent instantly. The smoke would make identification of a man almost impossible. Also, it might hide them completely; under its screen of darkness, the buildings could be torched. This latter was the worst. The smoke made identification impossible for Kalin and his men, too. Carl realized he had to make his move, and move fast.

He ran down the hill, drawing a bullet as he hurried. He saw the flame of the rifle, but he did not have time to shoot — the flame came from the edge of the smoke, about a hundred yards away. He plunged into the rolling, dark mass, and the smoke bit his nostrils, hot and thick. Yonder he could hear the dim crackle of burning brush, and through the smoke could be seen the flames, licking across the brush in the high wind.

A cottonwood tree toppled, showering sparks. It crashed to the ground, stock burned through, and it flared into violent color, then died down as swiftly as it had flared.

The smoke hung to the ground for most part, and then, without warning, a man would hit a clear spot, where the atmosphere, for a few feet, would have no smoke, this evidently being caused by pockets in the atmosphere. He ran toward the cabin. The cabin was the closest building to him.

He thought of the two women and the baby, in the root cellar.

Would the smoke suffocate them? This thought speared through him, and with it was the memory of Janet's cheery smile, her gay words, her temper, her loveliness. No, smoke went up, not down; the root cellar was dug into the earth. They could lie close to the earth and hug the cool sod and the smoke should, by all rights, go over them — also, there was but one opening to the root cellar, the section of log they had cut out.

Then another fear clutched him. Fire burned the oxygen out of air. Without oxygen, the human body could not exist. He remembered then a few years back: a forest fire had smashed across the Rockies, so the weekly newspaper had said, and a group of geologists, trapped by the fire, had hidden in a cave — only to die there when the fire had burned out their supply of oxygen. Would this happen to the women? And the baby?

Then this fear, too, was shoved aside by logic. There was no fire here — only smoke. Smoke could choke, bring out tears, tear the lungs with racking coughs, but the fire was too far away — it would not burn out the oxygen.

This was a good thought.

He was on the level area now, in the farmstead yard. From the north came a yipping yell and he heard, "Sodbuster, Sodbuster," and he recognized Shorty Madlin's voice.

It came from around the barn.

"Sodbuster," he hollered in return.

"Sodbuster over here," came back the cowpuncher's voice.

Carl felt the spearing lift of elation. Good old Shorty! He was coming in, rifle in hand, and fighting for the barn. Then, to the west, through the roiling, swirling smoke, came another man's voice — this was strident and wild with anger and ugliness.

"Sodbuster!"

That was John O'Reilly, moving down from his perch on the hill. Plunging into the smoke, rifle clutched in his grip, fighting for his wife, his baby, and his sister. Fighting for his own life.

"Sodbuster over here!" Carl hollered.

Shorty yelped, "Sodbuster over by the barn."

"Give them hell, sodbusters!" the farmer roared.

To his right, Carl heard a man snarl, "They're waiting for us, men. Burn your way through, or you don't collect a cent of wages!"

He knew that voice instantly. Had he not been able to identify it by its sound, he would have identified it by the words *a cent of wages*. Even in the stress of a gunfight, Matthew Kalin thought in terms of money.

Carl turned toward the voice. Over by the barn, rifles rang out, sharp and crackling. He could not see the flame of them for the smoke was too thick. The smoke rolled in, dense and stinging, and Carl went to his knees, coughing and with water streaming from his eyes. Kalin had played a good card when he had set the brush on fire. And the gods of chance, too, had been on his side. For the wind was blowing in the right direction to sweep the smoke across the farm yard.

So far, Carl had seen nobody; he had only heard voices. He worked his way toward the house, for the voice of Matthew Kalin had come from that direction. He had lost his sense of direction in the smoke — it was like being wrapped in black night. The wind blew in, a little harder; the smoke cleared, and he saw the watering-trough, there beside the pump. This gave him an idea. He ran to it and soaked his bandanna in the cool water, then held this to his nose to strain the smoke from the air. This helped him some. The water felt cool to his face. He heard the far dim crackle of burning brush, and he knew the fire was sweeping up the creek. Because he had found the watering-trough, from it he could judge the distance and direction of the house.

Again, from the direction of the barn the rifles talked. Shorty was really smoking it out with one of the Kalin men. Carl grinned wryly to himself. *Smoking* it out was really correct. He himself had done very little shooting; once he shot at what he thought was a man; it turned out to be the tie post in front of the house. Suddenly, out of the smoke, loomed the log cabin and Carl stopped, heart pounding.

A man was on the narrow porch, in the act of crossing it. The wind had come in, sweeping the smoke away. He could see the man clearly. He carried a rifle. He was wide and he wore a blue suit, even to a tie and white shirt. Despite the heat, his coat was on.

Carl said loudly, "Matthew Kalin, turn around and meet me, you damned cheap would-be murderer!"

There was, then, a moment's pause. Kalin seemed riveted to the dirt floor of the porch, his heavy body frozen in obese immobility. Carl had his rifle half-raised, and his eyes were on the man and on nothing else. The thought came that he hoped smoke would not streak in and break the clearness. And this wish was granted to him.

Matthew Kalin turned then, a big cat on big feet, and his rifle was rising. He was big and wide and he was a city man no longer; there was no softness, no flabbiness. He was hard and tough and fighting for his almighty dollar. His face was broad, the moonlight momentarily angling across it, giving it a cherubic look; yet, despite this deception, the face was stern and ugly.

"Carl Hudson, huh?"

Carl said, "Throw down your rifle and put up your hands. You'll never get away with it, Kalin. You hear me, don't you?"

"I sure do." Kalin was silent, then, watching him. Then, without another word, he brought his rifle up and, as he fired, he went to one broad knee, and he knelt there in the dust. He was fighting and he was tough.

Carl Hudson read the stark, ugly hatred there on the wide face. But still he remembered Birdie Kalin, and this man was her father. Mingled with these nasty thoughts was another thought: He had never killed a man, nor did he wish to ever kill one.

Later, he remembered with great clarity his gunfight with the millionaire, and when he later thought of the gun fight, each movement made had been clear and concise, correctly remembered. But now all the action came in blurred suddenness. He too went to one knee, and he brought his rifle up with a sweeping move that told of long practice.

The swiftness of his drop to his knee probably saved his life for the bullet of Matthew Kalin went over Carl Hudson. Then Carl's Winchester spanged sharply. The two rifle reports were almost one, Carl's behind Kalin's. He shot for Kalin's broad right shoulder. He shot for the point where the rifle stock jammed the thick shoulder.

And his bullet hit that spot.

The bullet smashed through the hardwood stock of the rifle. It ripped into Matthew Kalin's broad shoulder. It made Kalin grunt, and it made his eyes open in pain and in surprise. The bullet made him drop his rifle. The bullet drove him to his hands and knees, head down.

"Don't shoot!" Kalin screamed the words now. "I've dropped my rifle, Hudson — for Gawd's sake, don't shoot me!"

Carl got to his feet and came in, face savage with anger. He lifted his rifle barrel first and drove the stock down on the back of the banker's oak-like neck. Smoke skirled in, and the rifle's butt-plate made a hollow sound against the man's corded muscles.

And Kalin went down on his belly, knocked unconscious.

For a moment, legs spread wide, Carl stood over him. Smoke rolled in, hid him; then, the wind moved, and the smoke broke, leaving him outlined. He said, "That'll hold you, Kalin," and the harshness of his voice surprised even himself. He made to turn, thinking he would have to continue this grisly task, and then the hard push came from behind, striking him with unexpected hardness. Behind him he heard the roar of a pistol and he thought, Somebody has shot me.

He was down then, and he remembered rolling over, and he remembered the bullet hitting the dust, spouting dust over him. This seemed like a weird and uncertain nightmare, for the lines were not solid — they shifted and moved, blending into each other. Only one line was rigid; somebody had come in from behind him and shot him in the right ribs.

Then, he saw the gunman.

"Winn Carter," he said.

Carter stood there, legs wide; his face was ugly. Carl had dropped his rifle and he drew his six-shooter. Because of his wound, his draw was slow — it seemed an eternity before he got his gun from leather and before it sent out its first bullet.

During this time Carter shot again.

But Carl had sense enough to roll and Carter missed him. Carl was wild with fear and pain, and he shot twice. One shot missed but the other was lucky. The other saved his life.

Carl had seen death come before both to beast and man. But this was self-defense, and this wiped aside his scruples. He remembered that Carter had yelled something and then Carter was toppling. He dropped his gun and he walked ahead and then he fell in the dust and his nose was deep in the liquid earth. And he did not move. He did not even try to close his mouth, opened and filled with bloody dust.

Carl tried to get to his knees.

He couldn't.

The smoke moved in, making him cough. The next thing he knew he was on his back, looking up into the smoke. The world was getting smokier each minute. Just before he passed out he heard a roaring voice say, "You Bar T outlaws — surrender, savvy? This is the Law speaking . . ."

And then the smoke thickened and killed all vision, all feeling. His last thought was that the sheriff of Sulphur Springs had owned that roaring voice. Later, through the darkness, he heard a woman say, "He's coming out of it, folks."

Janet, Carl thought.

He opened his eyes. He was not out in the yard with the dead body of Carter a few feet away, with the unconscious millionaire lying in the dust. He was in the cabin on the bed and somebody had lit the kerosene lamp. Janet sat beside the bed, looking down at him.

Beyond her sat Shorty Madlin, right arm in a sling. Patsy stood beside the table, watching him, and holding the baby. That left only John O'Reilly to be accounted for.

"Where is John?"

From the other bunk came the voice of the farmer. "Over here on the bunk, Carl. Table is between us so you can't see us. I stopped a bullet in my shin. Busted my leg all to smithereens."

"My ribs . . . feel busted. Feels like the time that Midnight horse kicked me in the ribs . . ."

"They winged me," Shorty said.

Janet spoke now. "The sheriff got here. He looked at your ribs, Carl. Said they were broken. Then he and his posse — the posse was made up of farmers — took the prisoners to town."

"They didn't take two," Shorty said. "They buried them on the hill."

Carl looked at the face of his grinning partner. "Who else — beside Winn Carter?"

"Mike Hendricks."

"Oh."

Janet said, "This is one mess Kalin's money won't buy him out of, Carl. I wonder how he came to ride with his killers? I figured he would sit back like a general and order men around beyond the danger of bullets."

"His greed got the best of him," Carl said. "Talking is hard for me, so I won't do none more than I have to. Did the fire burn itself out?"

"All out, Carl. Hit the plowed area, then died."

"Oh my leg," groaned John O'Reilly.

His wife moved over and sat beside him, her face showing sympathy. The baby looked at the father with wide baby eyes.

Shorty said, "Sheriff'll throw the book at Kalin. Claimed up and down he would put Kalin behind bars for good. Sheriff said he would send the doc out from Sulphur Springs. Kalin said us farmers won't be bothered again by the Corporation. Say, you listenin' to your sidekick, Carl?"

Carl did not answer. He was looking for Janet. Her face was close, the lamplight showing its loveliness, and her lips were slightly open. She was looking at him and her eyes, there in the lamplight, were soft.

Shorty watched. John O'Reilly, despite his aching shin bone, got his weight on one elbow, and watched. Patsy watched. Only the baby didn't watch. He had a hand in his mouth looking at the ceiling.

Shorty said, "You can't pay attention to me, Carl — not when you kiss Janet like that . . ."

Finally Carl Hudson got free of Janet. He looked up at Shorty and winked. "I done hear every word you said," he lied.